Love Don't Love Me

3

by

Stacey Fenner

CONTENTS

Visit Stacey Fenner's Facebook for the latest news and updates.

Instagram: authorstaceyfenner

Twitter: @sfenner1

Facebook: www.facebook.com/authorstaceyfenner

DEDICATION

This book is dedicated to my cousin, Latarsha Barnes, who unexpectedly lost her husband resulting in a brief but wonderful marriage. Although I don't know your struggle, I see your struggle every single day. My prayer is that one day you can find the strength to open up your heart to love again.

Love will find you again, Tarsha! I believe that with everything in me.

R.I.P. Dante Barnes

Love you,
Stacey Fenner Blackwell

ACKNOWLEDGMENTS

First, I would like to thank God for guiding me through this journey of being an author. I couldn't be more grateful for my gift and for the fact that I've found my purpose in life.

A special thanks goes out to my cousin, Safiya Staggers, for gifting me her poetry.

To my good girlfriend, Relishia Payton Lynn—thank you for sharing your story with me!

As always, I want to thank you to my husband, Keith, my father, my two daughters, Jasmine and Janay, and my grandson, Nook, for loving and holding me down like you all always do.

A big thank you goes out to my family and friends. Your continued encouragement has helped push me to keep writing, even when I felt like giving up. I love you all more than words can even express.

Finally, I would like say thank you to my readers for your continued support. Words will never be able to express the appreciation I have for you.

CHAPTER 1

SAVONNA

FINAL FITTING

I stood in front of the mirror, admiring the custom wedding dress I'd had created for my big day, tears filling my eyes. We were only a week away from the finish line and my heart was filled with an overabundance of emotions.

Until I'd met Preston, I never thought I'd find a man who'd loved me enough to stick it out for the long haul. But with Preston…everything was different. He saw fit to make me his wife, placing a crown upon my head and setting me on throne like the queen he saw me as. Preston was a man who brightened my day even when we were having a disagreement. A man who showed me on a daily basis just how far he was willing to go to fight for us—how much he admired me. He's kind, caring, giving and he'd do anything to make me happy. Since meeting him, my life had changed drastically.

For the better.

After a lifetime of disappointment, it was finally time for me to find happiness. And I can honestly say that it had never felt better.

This heart of mine had been through a lot of turmoil over the years. So, looking back, it was hard to believe just how far I'd come to get to where I was now. When Preston entered my life, I thought it was too good to be true. Subconsciously, I was waiting for him to hurt me like all the rest, leaving me blowing in the wind. After nothing but years of bad luck when it came to love, what else was I supposed to think? Until that moment, I'd truly begun to believe that true love would never happen for me. Although I'd kept my heart open to the possibility of it, my confidence had been shattered. Somewhere deep down inside, I assumed I would end up being nothing more than a successful woman. *Alone.*

But I was wrong on so many levels.

Truth is, I had been selling my heart short for years. It took some time, but Preston made me realize that I deserved to get the love that I gave in return! I understand now that love can't be forced—no matter how bad I wanted it. Love is something that has to come naturally and that's exactly what happened to me. Despite the little voice in the back of my mind that told me it would all end soon, I trudged forward with every intention of enjoying the moment while silently praying that it wouldn't end!

I'd been through a number of men that had left me with a lot of false hope. Still, my heart told me that I had to go through each heartbreak in order to recognize true, unconditional love when it finally revealed itself. As time went on, my doubts about Preston vanished and I was finally able to face all my fears without feeling insecure. He's the most compassionate man that I'd ever encountered, supportive of anything that I do. One thing was for sure, he's definitely team Savonna. While I would have normally overlooked him in a crowd, it turned out that Preston was exactly the type of man I needed in my life.

From my bad experiences I'd learned to keep an eye on what a man values in life. And Preston's values—well, they set the stage for what type of man he really is. Even when he's lying to me, which isn't often, I can see past the bullshit. He's big on respect and never disrespects me no matter how mad I may make him.His acts of kindness towards others often remind me of myself. We have so much in common and he cherishes the same things that I do. We both look forward to coming home and snuggling with one another. We both love engaging in deep conversation, often losing track of time until the wee hours of the morning.

People often comment on our connection and how perfect we appear to be for one another. Little do they know, we are. Our personal metaphor is that I'm the cream to his coffee and he's the sugar to my tea. We laugh at it, but in all actuality it's pretty deep. It has a lot of meaning that only the two of us can understand.

"Savonna, you look absolutely gorgeous!" Angel, my Matron of Honor whispered, tears in her eyes as she looked at me in my wedding dress. All my alterations had been done to perfection and this was my final fitting before the wedding.

Some would say I went over the top by having this dress made, but I figured why not? The way I saw it, this was my forever and I didn't plan on doing it again. And since I'm only get married once—I figured I might as well get what I want. If you ask me, the dress was well worth the money I'd spent.

"Thank you. I know I shouldn't be, but I'm nervous."

We were down to the final days and I couldn't wait for everything to finally be over. I was exhausted. This experience did teach me one thing, I feel for every bride out there. Planning a wedding is like having another job. Thankfully, Angel has been a trooper from the get-go. Having gone through this three times, she knew every detail of wedding planning. She was certainly a better woman than me. One time was more than enough. And I hadn't even made it to the aisle yet.

Hiring Lucinda, a wedding planner, helped somewhat, but I still had to do the bulk of the work and I was still required to okay everything. You ask me, wedding planners are just another example of highway robbery. Lucinda called me every five seconds. It was driving me crazy. Last I checked, she was the wedding planner, not me.

"Don't you dare be nervous! You waited a long time for this. It's what you've always wanted." She squealed in excitement while wiping her eyes. "I can't wait. I wish I could blink my eyes and it be your wedding day! It's going to be epic." Preston was the first man that I'd been with that Angel actually approved of. You'd have thought she was the one that was getting married when I told her that he'd proposed.

"I know. I think I just put too much pressure on myself. I want everyone to say that this was the best wedding they've ever attended. The food has to be topnotch, no ugly dresses, the music needs to be right, decorations on point—all of it!"

Preston told me over and over again that I was putting too much emphasis on what other's thought and said about *our* wedding. I couldn't help it though, I'm a perfectionist all the way across the board. Last night, he told me that if I kept stressing, he was going to take me to the justice of peace.

"You can't please everyone, Savonna. But I'll tell you what…you won't get any complaints about this dress, Honey! When I say you're jaw droppingly stunning in that dress, I mean every word," Angel assured as she fixed the headpiece I was having problems with.

"Why wasn't I asked to be here?" Sky scolded, barging in unexpectedly and getting right to work straightening the bottom of my train. *This is why I didn't want her here,* I inwardly groaned.

Sky was known for being overbearing and wanted to have her nose in everything. At times, I feel like she was trying to recreate her own wedding to John. When she found out I'd asked Angel to be my Matron of Honor, she was pissed. For that very reason, I now have two. Sadly, that wasn't her attitude ended.

You should have seen her when she found out that I didn't want her and Samir to cater the reception. She damn near had a heart attack when she found out that my wedding was a black and white theme and that she was going to be wearing a black dress. Every decision that I made for my own wedding, she disapproved of. I couldn't remember a time we'd had so many disagreements.

"Because you, Tootie, and Mom were supposed to be getting final fittings done!" Little did she know, I'd made sure that their appointment would conflict with mine. I did it to keep them away from me. Tootie didn't bother me, but I didn't want to state the obvious. Not to mention, my mother wasn't too fond of my dress. She thought that it was too revealing. I just wanted to enjoy this moment without any distractions or extra opinions. It seemed that nearly everyone had forgotten that this was *my* wedding.

"When Mom told me you were here, I told them to get me in and out! I needed to be here for you." Sky took a step back and gasped. "And look how gorgeous you are in your dress!"

"Thank you. How did the fitting go?" I asked, hoping they managed to keep their dislike of Tootie under wraps.

Ironically, my choice of color scheme for the wedding was quite fitting given the family members involved. My mother and Tootie were like black and white themselves. Sometimes, when you mix tradition with non-tradition, it causes friction. I just needed to ensure that mommy-dearest and my overboard sister didn't get too carried away. When we first went to pick out the wedding party's dresses, my mother and Sky were acting very snobbish towards Tootie. They both claimed that Tootie had no class. Of course, I had to correct them.

Tootie was the most down to earth, well-educated person I'd ever met. Unlike them. Regardless of what they thought, or how they acted, not everybody was stuck up. If they'd have just hung around her long enough, they might have learned a thing or two without me having to interfere. Regardless, I was not going to have them treat my soon to be mother-in-law like an outcast. Like it or not, she was family.

"It went good—while I was there, at least. Don't worry, we were nice to Ms. Tootie," Sky scoffed, rolling her eyes.

"Vonna, we need to get you out of this dress," Angel insisted, changing the subject as she began unzipping me.

"Angel, I asked you to keep me informed," Sky seethed. "Wherever you go, I go!"

I rolled my eyes. *Here she goes, going off the wall again. I have no idea what's gotten into her, but she's getting on my last damn nerve.* Ever since we started planning this wedding, she kept trying to throw rank in Angel's face. Granted, Angel may not be related to me by blood, but she's just as much my sister as Sky.

"That's on me!" I interjected before Angel could speak. Lord knows that whatever was said would have turned into another argument. "I told Angel that you had to do your final fitting and wouldn't be joining us today." Truth be told, it was Angel's idea that I schedule both fittings at the same time. She knew I wanted it to be just the two of us and that I didn't know how to do it without hurting feelings. So, she came up with a plan.

"Why would you schedule it on the same day? It doesn't make sense! You know I wanted to be here." Sky was clearly upset. More than I would have ever expected her to be. Then again, she wasn't supposed to be here at all and I didn't feel like arguing with her. Especially today.

"Sky, it's not always about you! For once it's about me!" I screamed at her unintentionally. I didn't mean for it to sound so harsh, but I was tired. Tired of trying to make everyone happy!

"Wow!" she whispered, a look of shock on her face. "I'm sorry, Vonna. I just wanted to be there for you every step of the way. You have to understand that this is a joyous time for all of us. We've all been waiting on this day for so long. I just wanted to take some of the stress off of you and make sure that you and Preston had everything just the way y'all want it. Charge it to my heart for trying!" Without another word, Sky handed my dress to the seamstress and made her way to the store's exit.

My shoulders sank as I watched my sister walk away. While I understood what Sky was saying, I couldn't help that it felt like she was suffocating me. Still, despite her reasoning, I felt awful for coming down on her so harshly.

I should have known better. Sky wasn't coming up against me like I'd originally thought. She was just being her overprotective self. All she's been doing is trying to help and I've been so ungrateful.

There were so many people out there that wished they had a sister that was constantly riding with them. And here I had one that I didn't appreciate. No, she wasn't exactly keen on wearing a black dress. Then again, nobody was. It was a wedding, after all. As for her displeasure with me not wanting her to cook for the reception— well, I knew that all stemmed from her wanting to ensure that everything would taste good.

I needed to figure out a way to right my wrong. "Sky—Angel and I are going to meet you at your house when we've finished up here." At first, she seemed a bit hesitant, trying to brush me off because I'd hurt her feelings. Eventually, she nodded in agreement.

"I'd also really love it if you could make us lunch while we go over the details of my bachelorette party." Both Sky and Angel closed their lips tightly as if to stop themselves from saying anything. I was tickled pink. *They must have something big planned,* I thought in excitement. Funny part is I didn't even want a bachelorette party. The bridal party was more than enough for me.

At the moment, all I wanted was my wedding day!

Chapter 2

Samir

"Damn, Samir. Just think, you have to do this again in two weeks!" Jacobi said as we were picking up our tuxes.

"Yeah, I just hope you make yours!" Little did he know, I was scared as hell that I was going to be left at the altar trying to explain to a church full of people that Jacobi got cold feet. One minute, he was getting married. And the next, he wasn't.

Jacobi reminded me of a paranoid crackhead when it came to his wedding. He had every doubt in the world and all the what ifs! It was so bad that he had me believing that becoming a husband wasn't for him. But that's his decision and one I can't make for him. It was his wedding that was up in the air, after all.

"You should have a little more faith in me than that! One wedding at a time! I'll see you at the bachelor party on Friday! Keep in mind, if you don't do a good job on Preston's then you're fired from mine!" Jacobi laughed as he climbed into his car.

I just stood there shaking my head as Jacobi drove off. *How in the hell does he expect me to have faith in him? Especially given his constant back and forth,* I thought in disbelief. *Every time the wind blows, he changes his mind. I never know which way he's leaning.*

Just the other day Jacobi called me saying, *"Man, I don't know if I can do this."*

Each time he would change his mind I grew even more confused and frustrated. He and Tamela weren't arguing. In fact, they got along wonderfully. It was like he sat down, his mind swirling with thoughts, before eventually flying off the handle and talking himself out of getting married. Next thing I knew, I was left talking him off the ledge. It seemed the closer the big day got, the worse he became! For now, I just needed to leave that all in God's hands.

If you ask me, I believe he's just deathly afraid of commitment and he should have never proposed. Luckily, poor Tamela is blind to it all. Don't get me wrong, Tamela's great, but if she knew everything I knew, Jacobi wouldn't have a wedding to have cold feet over.

Preston and Jacobi were like night and day. When I'm chilling with Preston, he seems happy as shit to be marrying my sister. He praises Savonna, goes above and beyond to help her with the wedding planning. If Savonna isn't happy, he isn't happy. He does whatever he can to make sure that she has the wedding that she wants. Jacobi, on the other hand, I don't even think he knows the colors of his own wedding. Tamela did everything on her own. He was just the 'yes man,' agreeing to anything she wanted. I've never seen anything like it. Even when Cassey and I tied the knot—yes, she had the most say, but I played my part too.

*****

Preston's best friend, Miles, had flown in from Charlotte yesterday so that the two of us could put together the last-minute touches on the bachelor party that was set to happen in a few days. All I had to do was meet him at the Hamilton Hotel, which was where he was staying.

I didn't really know much about him and I had never met him, but we'd talked a number of times over the phone. I exited the suit shop, tux in hand, grinning as I walked down 14th Street. Strangers were stopping and wishing their congratulations, naturally assuming I was the groom. Not bothering to correct them, I simply replied with a thank you.

No one was happier than me that baby girl was finally getting wifed up. Even better, I actually had love for the dude she was marrying. In my lifetime of dealing with my sisters, it wasn't often that I approved of any of the men they were dating. But when it came to Preston, I felt really good about him. He was one of the good ones.

After getting to know him, Preston appeared to be a standup guy. Although if I were being honest, I thought he was some kind of crazy when he asked my father and I for our approval to propose. Until that moment I'd never met even him. I'd heard about him, but we'd never crossed paths. I remember thinking, *Fool, I don't know anything about you. And until I do, I'm not giving you my approval to marry my sister.*

And I didn't.

Pops, on the other hand, well, he sought out the Lord. Unfortunately, he hadn't received an immediate answer, so he told Preston that he was unable to give his approval at that time. Preston was obviously disappointed. I could hear it in his voice. Still, I commended him for even asking. In this day and age, it was almost unheard of. That one simple act earned him my respect.

Disappointed as he was, Preston let us both know that he had every intention of proposing, regardless of how we felt. He explained that as long as Savonna said yes, that was more than enough for him. At the end of the day, she would be the one spending the rest of her life with him. While Pops and I didn't like hearing it, we both knew he was right. When it came to who Savonna loved, neither of us had much say. Preston continued by saying that he would one day earn our approval, given time enough to get to know him. I respected him for that at the time and didn't read too much into it.

After that, I went on about my business, expecting to hear that Savonna was engaged. I knew there was no way Savonna would ever say no. This was something she had been waiting for her entire life. Since we were kids, she dreamt of getting married. As an adult, she always said she felt like she's missing out on something. It was as if it were a completion to her life. So, when Sky called with the happy news, I wasn't surprised in the least.

What did surprise me, however, was that Preston kept his word. Instead of hiding in the shadows of my sister, he came around and made himself known to the entire family. It was like he was telling us that we all might as well get used to him because he wasn't going anywhere. And he didn't.

Preston made frequent visits to the house asking for martial advice. While I advised him on things from my perspective, I also told him that the real soldier was Pops. Come to find out, he was already picking his brain. According to Preston, he was getting the best information on old school and new school marriage. I liked that. Because Preston and I were from the same era, he would more likely be able to relate to my experiences, while still getting the wise counsel from Pops.

When we spoke, I didn't hold anything back. I gave him the whole ugly truth about being married. Like anything, I told him that a successful marriage was going to take work. Truth be told, it was one of the hardest jobs he would ever have in his life—besides raising kids. I told him that at some point in their marriage he may be tempted to stray, want to leave a million times, but that he needed to push forward and be ready for the battlefield. Regardless of what anyone thinks, nothing is perfect when it comes to marriage. It isn't always happy. No matter how wonderful things may seem at the moment, they will go through seasons where they bump heads and have some rocky times.

In the end, anybody can get married. The key is to stay married. I shared my story with Preston in hopes that it would help him in his own marriage. Either way, I assured him that I was here anytime he needed me. Over time, he got his approval to marry Savonna from me and Pops, just like he said he would.

Yet, regardless of how cool we were—and we were cool—he needed to see the other side of me. The side that would never allow him to hurt my sister.

He needed to see Savonna's brother.

I'd overlooked a lot of mess with my other two sisters, but I vowed to never let that happen with Savonna. I was taught to stay out of people's marriages, family included, and I had every intention of continuing to do that as best I could. That being said, under the right circumstances I was willing to break that rule in order to protect my sister. Preston assured me that I had nothing to worry about and I believed him. Still, he needed to know that I was watching, waiting for him to step out of line.

*****

"You must be the infamous Samir?" Miles greeted me with a hug in the hotel lobby. I must admit, it felt good to put a face to the voice. We had talked several times over the phone in an attempt to get this bachelor party together. He knew Preston better than me, so his input was very much appreciated. From my understanding, the two men are equivalent to me and Jacobi.

"That would be me. Good to finally meet you! How did you pick me out of this massive crowd?" I asked. There were so many people in the lobby, there was no way he knew that it was me. Unless, of course, he's a genius. But we both knew the odds of that were slim.

"Good to finally meet you, too. Preston sent me a picture so that I would know who to look for. I'm not psychic, if that's what you're thinking!" Miles laughed.

"You had me scared for a minute there!" I muttered, joining him in laughter.

"Have you talked to Preston today? He's not answering any of my calls!" Miles asked, glancing at his phone.

"Man, he's been so busy trying to get that house together. He probably just left his phone at the apartment. Come on, we'll drive over there."

I'd advised the two soon-to-be newlyweds to wait until after the wedding to purchase a home. But no, Savonna just had to close on a house and get married all at the same time. Preston, of course, agreed, willing to give her anything he could. Sadly, that now left him scrambling to try and get the house ready for after the wedding. Luckily for him, I'm off this week. And with Miles in town, the three of us could help him get it finished.

"I told him he was doing too much. He knows how he gets when he's overwhelmed. That damn house could have waited!" *I knew I wasn't crazy—Miles sounds just like me.*

The two of us hurried to my car and headed over to Savonna and Miles' new house. Unfortunately, given the time of day, we ended up stuck in afternoon DC traffic. Miles and I talked like we'd known each other for years. During our conversations, I found out a few things that I didn't know about Preston.

Apparently, he been down this road before with Preston. Evidently, Preston was previously engaged. A month before the wedding his fiancé called it off. Miles didn't elaborate, he was just happy that this wedding was happening. *I'll have to get that scoop from Preston at a later date,* I mentally noted.

At one point in time, Preston even tried his hand at basketball. Another thing he failed to disclose the entire time he had been with my sister. *Miles shouldn't have told me that. Now I have to challenge him to a game.*

"I told you he was here," I said as we pulled up to the house. "Go on in through the back, man. I'll be right in. I just have to check in with the wife real quick!" I watched as Miles headed toward the back of the house while I called Cassey.

"Hey, Babe, did you get your tux?" Seems that since we got married, Cassey thinks she's my mother. I mean, what the hell else would I be doing?

"Yes, Ma'am. I'm actually with Miles now. He seems like a pretty cool dude!" Panicked, I turned around to double check that I had hung up my tux and didn't accidently leave it in the hotel lobby.

"Aww, that's good. I'm over here at Mom's helping to put the wedding favors together. What time do you think you'll be done?" *Oh Lord, I hope she didn't make any plans.*

I told Miles that after we were finished here, we would hit up the strip clubs to pick out some ladies for the bachelor party. I needed them for Jacobi's bachelor party next week anyway, so I figured two birds, one stone. Originally, I'd suggested we keep the party clean. I kept imagining Preston running from the strippers. However, Miles objected profusely! Truth be told, I think he just wanted to see his friend's reaction.

"I'm going to be a while. The boys and I going to have some drinks a bit later," I explained, putting it mildly. I couldn't tell Cassey what I was really going to be doing because she'd blow the whole spot up.

"Uh huh. Showing off for Miles, I see!" Cassey laughed knowingly.

Just then, Miles came running from the house, screaming at the top of his lungs. "SAMIR! SAMIR! SAMIR!"

CHAPTER 3

SKY

I felt like I'd just woken up from the worst type of nightmare. *This can't be real life. I just need to go back to yesterday—back to when things were right.* My head felt like somebody had hit me with a brick, my heart was beating erratically, and I was shaking like a bat out of hell as tears streamed down my face.

The entire emergency room was filled with friends and family, not a dry eye in sight. All I could hear in between my own sniffles were those of everyone else's around me. The image of Tootie screaming and yelling, "Wake up, son! Wake up!" while pulling on Preston's shirt as paramedics were trying to rush him to the back would haunt me for the rest of my life.

Samir, God bless him, had Savonna thrown over his shoulder and she was beating the hell out of him while shouting, "PRESTON!

PRESTON! PRESTON!" I felt so helpless as I looked in both directions and saw heartbreak.

I vaguely recall seeing Angel running towards me with a frantic expression on her face. "What happened, Sky?" she shouted. "Sky!" I remember staring at her, too numb to answer. No matter how hard I tried, I couldn't seem to get my body, nor my mouth to cooperate. Undeterred, Angel reached over and grabbed me by the shoulders and began to shake me. "Sky, what happened? I need you to tell me what happened?" Still, I couldn't find the words. I was still in a state of shock and too weak to talk.

Just then, Samir rushed past me with Savonna's limp body in his arms and he was screaming, "NURSE! NURSE, HELP ME! PLEASE, MY SISTER!"

I watched in a haze as Angel rushed toward Samir, her voice panicked. "Samir what's wrong with Vonna? Vonna? Vonna? VONNA!"

I felt like I'd been standing in the same spot for hours before John ran up and pulled me into his arms while carefully leading me to a nearby chair. Beside me, Serenity was in tears, staring out the window looking lost. I'd been so distracted by my own grief that I didn't even realize she'd come in.

"SKY, PLEASE TELL ME HE'S NOT DEAD!" she shouted. "TELL ME HE DIDN'T DO THIS TO OUR SISTER! FUCKING COWARD! THAT FUCKING COWARD!" Before I could say anything, Jacobi came from out of nowhere, picked Serenity up, and carried her out of the emergency room.

When Samir returned a few minutes later—shirt torn and covered in dried blood—it looked like he'd just gone ten rounds with Floyd Mayweather. I could tell he was struggling to hold onto to what little strength he has remaining. In all my years, I'd never seen him needing support from others. Normally, it was the other way around. And in this case, his wife, Cassey, was the one trying to hold him together.

I could only imagine what the ride to hospital must have been like between after telling Savonna what had happened. It was bad enough he had to be the one to go get her and deliver the news. But to make matters worse, she happened to be at the surprise bridal party her co-workers at the practice had thrown.

Why my sister, Lord? I silently prayed. *Out of everybody in the world, why would you choose her? Hasn't she already been through enough? What will life look like for her when all is said and done?*

Everywhere I looked all I could see were painful faces. However, there was one in particular that grabbed my attention, one I hadn't seen before.

On the other side of the room, sitting across from Jacobi, was a strange man that I didn't recognize. From where I was sitting, I could see he was having a major breakdown. My heart immediately broke for a man I didn't even know and I couldn't bring myself to watch any longer. Looking away, I did my best to deal with my own pain. Unfortunately, even though I wasn't looking at him, I could still hear his broken-hearted sobs.

Someone either needs to take him out of here or I need to step outside, I thought to myself, unsure how much more I could take before breaking down again myself. Just as I prepared to stand, I remembered that I couldn't leave. *I need to be here when the doctor comes out.*

As if sensing my inner turmoil, I watched as my father strolled over to where the stranger sat. *I wonder what he's going to say,* I wondered, knowing there were no words that could comfort any of us.

My mom, the family rock, sat in dismay. Here we were, needing all the prayer we could get, and the prayer warrior was silent. After I got the call, I somehow managed to hold it together long enough to call my parents and tell them to get to the hospital. Before they could say anything, I hung up, leaving them in the dark about what they would be walking into. Though I'm pretty sure this latest tragedy didn't even enter their minds.

I'll never forget the look on my mom's face the moment they found out what had happened. My mother's legs gave out and my dad had to hold her up, a look of terror on both of their faces. I wouldn't wish something like this on my worst enemy. One thing was for sure, in order for us to get through this, it was gonna require that we all lean on one another for support.

Especially when it came to Savonna.

*****

Everyone jumped up as the doctor came out with an update. Me, I remained sitting, unable to make my legs work. "Are you all the McMillan family?"

"YES!" everyone shouted in unison.

"First off, Ms. McMillian is fine. Her vitals are stable, but we did have to sedate her to keep her calm. That being said, I would like to keep her under observation for twenty-four hours. I suggest you all go home and come back tomorrow. However, if you do choose to remain here in the hospital, you are more than welcome to stay in the family room," he explained, waiting for a reply.

"Danielle and I will stay," Angel said, volunteering herself and her wife. "Y'all go home and get some rest. If anything changes, I'll call." *They can leave because there is no way I'm going anywhere. When my sister wakes up, she will see my face,* I thought to myself in anger.

John tried talking me into going home, but I refused. Home didn't need me, this hospital did. And so did my sister. I knew that if I went home, the only thing I would do is drive myself crazy waiting for the phone to ring by a non-family member. Angel may be Vonna's best friend, and I respect that, but in the event of an emergency, she couldn't make medical decisions on her behalf. Which is precisely where Angel and I butt heads. She tends to forget her place. Little did she know, our parents would never allow her to be here without at least one of us.

As expected, Serenity also refused to leave. Luckily, she was responsible enough to call Profit and ask him if he would he keep Lil Sky while she stayed at the hospital. When she hung up with him, she gave Gary a courtesy call. He was supposed to be bringing the kids back home by eight. Given the circumstances, he agreed to keep them for as long as she needed. She and Savonna still weren't on the best of terms, but she wasn't leaving her sister's side either. And Lord knew I needed her with me.

Despite everyone's desire to remain by Savonna's side, they knew there was nothing they could do for her. Only time would tell how everything played out. With a group prepared to remain at the hospital, in case of emergency, everyone else decided to head home until morning. Samir appeared too shook to drive, so Cassey took Samir home and Jacobi followed her in his car. While we'd all had a rough day, Samir and Miles had the most challenging—being the ones to find Preston. I didn't really know Miles, but I'd heard through conversation that he was Preston's best friend. Which explained his complete breakdown earlier.

Tamela met Jacobi at Samir's house and brought him back to the hospital so he could pick up Miles and drive him back to his hotel. Miles was hesitant, so it took a little convincing. Eventually, Jacobi got him in the car and made sure he made into his hotel room safely. While Jacobi was getting Miles secured in his hotel room, Tim and his wife, Camille, went home with the assurance that they would be back first thing in the morning.

Nicole, who was the first to go home, asked that I call her with any updates. Chad, who I hadn't seen in ages, decided to show his face when he heard what had happened. He remained at the hospital until they moved us all into the family room. Which is about the same time that everyone else headed home.

Everyone except our parents.

Mom and Dad didn't want to leave Savonna's side, understandably. It took all of us to convince them to go home and get some rest. I assured them that I would call if anything were to arise. My only hope was that I wouldn't need to contact them.

"I wonder how Tootie is doing," I muttered. I didn't know much about her, but I prayed she wasn't alone. Last I saw, she was running out of the hospital and she hadn't been back since. One thing was for sure, she was going to need some support. Losing a child was painful enough, but to lose your only child was absolutely devastating.

"Who cares, Sky," Serenity snapped, jumping up from the recliner she'd been lounging on. *Here she goes again—being her normal insensitive, selfish ass.*

"That's not at all fair, Serenity! Whether we like her or not, that woman lost a child!" Angel countered.

"Don't come at me with that bullshit! Y'all act like Preston got killed or died from a deadly disease! The motherfucker hung himself a week before marrying our sister! Why are we dancing around the real reason we're all in this situation right now?" Serenity began pacing the floor, throwing punches in the air and breathing in and out like a crazed person.

"I'm glad you said it because I was thinking the same damn thing!" Danielle agreed. "He's wherever the hell he is and we're all left here, hurting! Shit ain't right!"

"I get that, but it still doesn't negate the fact that Tootie didn't deserve this." I didn't disagree with Serenity or Danielle, but this wasn't Tootie's fault either. She didn't ask for this. No one in their right mind would ask for their child to be found dead. Especially like that.

"We're all entitled to our own opinions, but now is not the time. We have to come up with a game plan for when Savonna comes off this sedation. We all know that she's strong, but can she survive this?" Angel asked, a look of concern etched across her face.

"That's why I'm so damn angry!" Serenity snapped. "She always gets dealt a shitty hand. I mean, how much more can she take?" She sounded like she'd lost complete faith in our sister. I wasn't naïve enough to think this wasn't going to be difficult for her. But I also knew my sister…she's stronger than anyone believes her to be.

"We have to think positively. She's still among the living and has a lot of life in her!" I glanced up at the clock to check the time. Time was moving so slowly and it felt like we'd been here all night. I guess you could say I was anxious to see my sister again.

"Sky, let's be realistic here. We haven't even begun to unravel the depth of this horrible situation and the chain of events that have been set off because of it. Instead of a wedding, we all now have a funeral to attend. One that I'm sure Savonna will foot the bill for because you and I both know that there isn't a life insurance company out there that will cover suicide. And that doesn't even begin to touch the fact that there are cancelation notices for the wedding that have to go out. Add to that, the questions that Savonna may never get answers to in regards to Preston's death. Then there are the more pressing questions—is she going to live in the house they just purchased together? The same house her fiancé was just found dead in. That's a lot for anyone. I know Savonna better than all of you and I know she's going to blame herself for his death. She's not going to want to live without him!"

While Angel made some valid points, I intended to take it one day at a time. Anything more than a day was too far ahead for me. While I could have chosen to be offended by her last remark, I let her have it. The sad truth is that Savonna did share more with her than she did with us. I suppose you could say it was one of the side effects of our strained relationships. For the moment, though, I intended to lay here and play the waiting game.

CHAPTER 4

SERENITY

When Savonna came out of sedation there was no calm to her storm. Especially once she realized that it wasn't all just a terrible nightmare. That's when all hell broke loose. I was standing at the foot of her bed, Angel and Danielle to the right, and Sky to the left. I don't know if I'll ever forget the look on her face as she cried out in agony. To see her so emotionally broken, hurt beyond measure, just intensified my own mental struggles.

While I'd spent most of my days laying low since everything transpired, I still tried to send a thoughtful, encouraging text to Savonna every day. I knew she wasn't in the mood for any deep, meaningful conversation, so I did my best to keep our conversations brief. I figured she would come to me when she was ready.

Everyone thought they had all the answers to what Savonna needed, but I was the only one who truly understood what she was going through. I tried to tell Sky not to crowd and clutter up her space, to let her breathe if she didn't want to be the one she lashed out at. And what do you think happened? Sky did exactly what I told her not to do and Savonna cursed Sky out just like I said she would. Pressuring her to eat and sleep, two things she wouldn't do, was the last thing she wanted to hear.

No one seemed to understand that this wasn't just your usual heartbreak. This was traumatic. And because of that, it was going to take extensive therapy for her to get back to anything that even remotely resembled normal. She wasn't just going to wake up one day and be okay.

You would think, after everything, that my family would come to me for advice. But no, they still couldn't give me enough credit. Little did they know, trauma was a world of its own. It was different from grief and unfortunately, Savonna was dealing with both.

Preston's funeral was one of the worst that I'd ever been to. Normally, I wouldn't have even gone, but I wanted to support my sister. Looking back, I'm glad I went because it gave me clarity as to why Savonna loved him so much.

I didn't know Preston that well because Savonna and I had been on the outs for most of their relationship. However, from the moment I stepped inside the crowded church, which was standing room only, it was clear that the man had touched many lives and done a lot for the community. It appeared to be a great loss for everyone in attendance. And Mother Nature agreed.

It was a dreary day in DC, dark clouds with no rain in sight—a perfect representation of the mood. I always paid attention to the weather because I found there to be so much meaning behind it. The problem is that people rarely bothered to dig deep enough to discover that meaning. A fact which I found to be quite ironic.

That was the day I learned just how giving Preston was. He donated his time and money to all types of community projects. Though his soft spot was for children and single mothers. Apparently, he'd received a number of awards for his services throughout his life. His EMT partner, Derek, got up and spoke about how Preston would always go above and beyond his job description. He mentioned how Preston would double back to the hospital to check on the patients or the families that were in mourning after he was off shift. That's how much he cared.

Though he speech that really struck me was the one his best friend, Miles, gave. He spoke about how very few people knew just how bad Preston suffered from depression. How, despite him knowing about his depression, he still didn't see the signs. According to Miles, this was the happiest he'd ever been. Through his tears, he urged anyone that suspected they were battling this deadly disease to seek the help that they needed. He also reiterated that it was important to continue treatment because even when you think you're fine, depression can creep up without notice. To be honest, I was still trying to figure it all out. None of it made any sense.

After I got shot, I had my own battle with depression, but nothing made me want to hang myself. I had three children to take care of and one in my stomach that was going to need me. That alone kept me afloat. Now, that's not to say I didn't have bad days because I did. Whenever I felt like I was losing my battle, I would call my therapist and lean on my children.

For the life of me I couldn't figure out what could have triggered Preston to commit suicide? He had a seemingly wonderful life—the kind of thing many people spend a lifetime looking for. He had a mother that adored him, and a fiancé that he was madly in love with. Knowing that he was headed to the altar in just a few days should have been enough to outweigh his depression. Sadly, that wasn't the case. Of course, I understand that weddings can be stressful, but he had very little responsibility in that respect. His only job was to show up. I know things affect people differently but damn, I hate him for doing this! Not only to my sister, but to the rest of the family. I just wish I could bring him back for five minutes to ask him why? I just wanted to understand what was going on in his head. Perhaps it would help me help Savonna.

Staring at my bridesmaid dress, I began to wonder what I was going to do with it. Deep down, I knew Savonna wouldn't want us to keep them. It would just be another sad reminder of what would have been. *Maybe I can donate it to a local high school senior that's in need of a prom dress,* I thought as my mind drifted back to everything that had happened for Savonna and I to get to this point.

Truth be told, I almost didn't make the cut for the wedding party. It was a last-minute decision on Savonna's part. I had been talking to Sky about how I didn't want to be left out and she convinced Savonna to talk to me, claiming it was time to end the feud. This was a milestone in my sister's life that I would cherish for the rest of my life. Sisters fight–it's natural–but Savonna was taking this to the extreme. My kids missed her and the only reason she had met her new niece was because Sky had her at the time.

In the end, Savonna agreed to meet me at Sky's house for a sit down. At first, it was very awkward. We quickly found ourselves right back to where we'd left off, arguing and not making any progress. Bless her, Sky was trying to be the mediator but the conversation grew more heated with each passing minute. It's hard to make someone see your side when they feel the way they feel and you feel the way you feel. That being said, she needs to understand that nobody can run my life. It's my life to live and I don't owe her an explanation for the way in which I choose to live it. Regardless of my reasoning, I knew she would never understand why I choose to talk to a maniac.

It took a while, but we eventually came to a mutual understanding. She wouldn't bring up Iron and neither would I. I did apologize for the hurtful things that I said to her and we were able to move on from there. While I was glad to have the rift between us mended, I knew right then that we would never be as close as we once were. I was used to being able to talk to Savonna about anything and that was no longer going to be the case.

Savonna and I left Sky's house together and went back to mine so that she could see the kids. She ended up spending the rest of the day with us. While she was with us, I made sure to ignore Iron's phone calls in an effort to avoid any confusion. We ended up having a good time, horsing around, before eventually cooking dinner together.

Ironically, that was the first time I met Preston. He'd come over for dinner. To my surprise, the kids took to him right away. They had a ball. When they had finished eating, Savonna fed Lil Sky and put her to bed for the night while Preston put the other three to bed. I had just finished cleaning up the kitchen when they reappeared. I poured us each a glass of the wine Preston had brought over and the three of us sat down in the living room to watch Act like a lady, Think like a man. We'd all seen it at least a half of a dozen times, but it was still just as good as the first. By the time they left to head home, it was nearly two in the morning.

One thing that night showed me was just how much I missed my sister. It had been so long since I'd had that much fun. And it felt like even longer since I'd hung out with Savonna.

It felt like I'd waited an eternity on pins and needles for Savonna to ask me to be in their wedding. While, in reality, it had only been two weeks, I was expecting her to ask me right away. Naturally, I assumed she was taunting me. When I finally said something about it, she actually had the nerve to laugh about it. Which, of course, I didn't find funny at all. Since we hashed things out, she had been sharing all the details of the wedding with me but never asked me to be in it.

Finally, the day of the first fitting for the bridesmaids, she asked if I would be one of her bridesmaids. As soon as she gave me the details, I hauled ass to the store to meet Danielle and Cassey with my deposit in-hand. If this were any other day, I wouldn't have been prepared. But this wasn't any other day and I was prepared.

After everything I had gone through, there wasn't even going to be a wedding. And now I felt shorted. I know that sounds terrible, given the fact that I wasn't the bride and my sister lost her fiancé, but I couldn't help how I felt. Don't get me wrong, my heart ached for Savonna. No one, man or woman, should have to experience the loss of their significant other just days before their wedding day. If you ask me, it ranks right up there with losing a child.

RING! RING! The sound of the telephone ringing pulled me from my thoughts.

As soon as I picked up the phone the stupid recording from the prison began to play. *Iron must have decided to call earlier than usual,* I thought to myself before accepting the charges.

"Hey, Bae," I greeted.

"What up, were my baby at?" Iron asked, finally acknowledging that Sky was his. Normally, he would just say, *"Where that baby at?"* However, given the recent DNA test, he didn't have much of a choice but to accept it. Of course, there was never any doubt in my mind that he was the father. The moment I saw the birthmark on her little foot, I knew. It's the same as his. Unfortunately, Iron wouldn't take my word for it.

"She's sleeping, thank God!" Sky's teeth were starting to come in, so she was being unbearable. Thankfully, the Tylenol was helping to keep the fever down, but I could only put Anbesol on her mouth so many times. It was days like this that made me want to hit myself upside the head for starting over.

"Wake her up. She needs to hear my voice, yo!" Iron said. He was so ghetto, but I loved him regardless.

"No, absolutely not! She can hear your voice tomorrow." Normally, I would have woken her up just to see her smile, but today was not going to be one of those days. Any time she heard Iron's voice she would smile and coo, as if she knew that he was her daddy. Since he couldn't be here to see how much she changed from day to day, I would send him pictures of her often. One minute she looked like me, the next she looked like him. I couldn't believe how grown up she looked now. It seemed like just yesterday I had given birth to her.

"Aight, I'll let it slide this time. Yo, did you get that license?" Before I could answer, I heard the CO's put him back on lockdown and the line disconnected. *I'll be glad when his bid is over,* I inwardly groaned. It seemed every time I turned around, they were on lockdown. He normally called every day, so I knew what had happened anytime I didn't hear from him. I didn't even need to question it.

Iron and I recently decided to get married while he's in jail. I couldn't believe that I was going to be having another jail wedding. Then again, it didn't really matter to me where I got married. Truth is, no one would come anyway. Neither of us had told our family. I knew mine was going to have a fit, regardless. And his family—well, they blame me for him being in there in the first place. I'm sure there will be plenty of backlash when they find out.

I can hear them now, *'How could she?' 'How could he?'* The list goes on and on. We were both expecting to be disowned, but neither of us cared. We're both adults and had a right to live our lives the way we saw fit. Regardless of what other people thought.

And when it comes to my family—I had no intention of telling them until Iron was released. If he stays on the good foot, he'll be out in two more years. I get lonely sometimes, but the only thing that gets me through is the fact that I know it won't last forever.

My greatest concern is for my kids. Their feelings are the only ones that matter to me. I told Iron when we decided to get married that he was going to have to take baby steps when dealing with them. He would have to regain their trust. He agreed. I decided I would try to slowly ease them into the thought of it. Since they were already aware that I talked to him, I didn't think it would be that hard. Of course, they assumed we only spoke because of the baby. Unfortunately, I had a feeling that I would have one stubborn child. And I was correct.

Serene was proving to be the hardest to get through to. She just couldn't understand why he needed to call at all. Each day, I found myself patiently explaining the same thing to her over and over again. It had become so verbatim that she now finished my sentences. My only hope is that Jesus will be able to fix this and open everyone's heart up to forgiveness.

It was a process for me to forgive Iron. One that didn't happen overnight. We had conversation after conversation and wrote one another back and forth. At one point, I received a letter every day, no less than four pages. It took a lot of understanding on both our parts. After a while, I came to the realization that I cared for Iron, but I never truly loved him. It wasn't until we couldn't see each other and I was left with only the words he wrote on paper that I fell in love with him. With me, he's an entirely different person.

After everything I had been through in life, I finally understood that people change. And Iron was no different. The man lives with the regret of what he did every day of his life, and apologizes often. When I speak to him or read one of his letters, I don't even consider him to be the man that shot me.

I know that no one will understand where I'm coming from, and I accept that. It's far too complex to understand unless it happened to you. My only hope is that they, too, will come to accept it. For me.

In a way, Iron being locked up ended up being the best thing to happen to us. For the first time, possibly ever, we were in a good place and because of that we had big plans once he was released. Both of us were tired of DC, so we decided we were going to move to Atlanta once we got his parole transferred. In the meantime, he would start working on getting his CDL. If everything went as planned, Iron would finally be able to afford to take care of us when he finished school.

Given the price of daycare these days, we decided it would be financially prudent if I continued to collect my disability and remain at home with the baby. Once Sky was in school full time, I'd be able to make a career move. While I'm still undecided at the moment, I figured that would give me the time to figure out what my niche is. Assuming I can even work again.

I still have my bouts of anxiety and suffer from night terrors. According to my therapist, that's just my new normal and it will likely never go away. I refuse to accept that. So, for now, I'm just going to take it one day at a time. If the good Lord has a plan for me to go back to work, He will make sure it happens.

CHAPTER 5

SAMIR

Two days after the funeral I somehow managed to pull myself together enough to get through Jacobi's wedding. Seeing Preston like that, days before his own wedding was a hard pill to swallow, but I knew I had to bite the bullet and put on a hell of a façade for my friend. It's no joke being a man sometimes, trying to hold your composure in the face of tragedy. I made it look good though. At least on the outside. Inside, I was bursting at the seams, tears begging to break free.

While I was happy for my boy, I was in mourning for my sister's loss. Fake smiles and forcing myself to laugh, while at times choking up—it was like I was waging war with myself, fighting to not lose my manhood. There was no way I could allow myself to show any vulnerability in front of two hundred people. Thankfully, the only two people that noticed my inner turmoil were Cassey and

Jacobi. Rightfully so, since they knew me better than I even knew myself.

I kept my best man speech short and to the point so that I didn't stumble over my words and cause everything I'd been holding inside to bubble to the surface. "First off, I would like to make a toast to Tamela for taking this dude off my hands. Marriage is work; I won't even begin to lie about that. But just remember, when times get tough–and they inevitably will–it's important to have someone in your corner. I am that someone. If you ever need me, day or night, my phone is always on and I will be here to hold you both up. Welcome to the family, Tamela!" When I had finished, the inner kid in me glanced over at Pops, who nodded his head in approval.

I don't know why, perhaps it was everything that had happened over the last week, but I felt like I needed his reassurance just as I did when I was growing up. Funny how, as a grown man, I reverted back to my childhood days, looking to my father for his approval. I guess that's what happens when you're struck with such a traumatic experience.

For generations it's been said that men aren't supposed to cry. I suspect that came about from the old ideal that men were the pillar of the household, expected to carry the load of the family. However, the way I was feeling today was making it hard to uphold that old adage.

I normally did my best to keep my tears private, but today they were threatening to spill over for the entire world to see. Though you know what the worst thing about it was? The fact that I felt like a complete hypocrite in front of my son. Any time he would fall or get a little bruise, I would tell him to wipe his tears and man up. Yet, here I was, having a hard time keeping my own emotions at bay. It was something I'd never experienced. My entire life I'd been the one to keep myself and everyone else around me together. So, how could I call myself a man when I was internally struggling?

Growing up, Pops prepared me for damn near everything life could throw at me. But he never prepared me for moments like this. What's one supposed to do in times like this? I wasn't sure. One thing I was sure about–as I had learned it firsthand–unaddressed issues led to more underlying issues. Life brought enough trouble of its own and I didn't want to be the type of man that ran to drugs, alcohol, sex, and women in an effort to suppress the truth. Self-sabotage was not the direction I wanted to go.

This trial in my life had me so perplexed. I couldn't go to the gym and bench press two hundred pounds or run some lay ups to let off some steam. I couldn't throw up a couple of beers and a nip to ease the pain. Truth is there was no fix for the nightmares and images that constantly surfaced in my mind. I was walking on troubled waters that I didn't know how to navigate. For a moment, I contemplated therapy, but that ain't me. I'm a black man—what would it look like if I started talking to a shrink? Not that they would be able to help me anyway. No one would be able to help me until they've walked a mile in my shoes.

It's for that reason I keep in frequent contact with Miles. He's just like me…he's faking it. He may not realize it, but I can read between the lies. He may say he's all right, but I know better.

There's no way, not after seeing the same thing that I saw. His emotions had to be all over the place.

I'll never forget the look on his face as he came running from the house, screaming my name in total agony. I didn't even hang up the phone before jumping out of my car and running towards the backyard to help him. I thought maybe a tree had fallen on Preston or something. It wasn't until I reached the garage that I came to an abrupt halt as what looked like Preston's body hanging from the rafters came into view.

I could feel the blood drain from my face as Miles' screams faded until it resembled a whooshing in my ears. Perhaps it was because I was in a state of shock, but my body felt paralyzed. I couldn't move. I don't know how long I stood there staring at Preston's suspended body before the neighbors, having heard the screams, came running over. The moment they laid eyes on him, they called 911.

At first, I wanted to believe that someone else had done this to him. I *needed* to believe that someone else had done this. I needed someone else to blame other than the man I was fixing to call my brother. In the back of my mind I was certain the man I had grown to know would never go out like this. He loved my sister too much. I would even venture to say he loved her more than he loved himself. It was undeniable affection that anyone who ever met them could see. I truly believed there was no way he could be this selfish. He didn't even leave a suicide note.

It didn't take the police long to rule out any signs of foul play, but I was still having a hard time believing that my friend, supposed to have been brother-in-law, was capable of taking his own life.

Preston and I checked in on one another daily. The night before we found him, he was talking about excited he was to see Miles. He seemed ecstatic to finally be marrying my sister and was looking forward to his bachelor party. For the life of me I couldn't figure out what had changed in less than a day. Unfortunately, we'll never know now because he's not here to tell us.

I remember looking at my phone the day before and seeing a text that let me know he was checking in and wanted to hang out.

PRESTON: What's up, Bruh? What's the rest of your day looking like?

Since he'd first asked to marry my sister, we had grown quite close. He'd became the brother that I'd never had in such a short time. And now, he was gone. Shit still hasn't sunk in. It just didn't sit right with my soul and I wasn't sure that it ever would.

After we had finished answering the officer's questions, we attempted to compose ourselves before leaving to do the impossible. We had to notify the rest of the family. Starting with Savonna and Preston's mother, Tootie.

While Miles went to notify Tootie, I was left to go and deliver the bad news to Savonna who was attending her surprise bridal party that her work had thrown her. As soon as I walked in and she saw my face she knew that something was wrong. Naturally, she assumed that something had happened to one of our parents. Little did she know, the last person on her mind, the man that she was about to marry was a victim of his own making.

It took all the strength I could muster to tell my sister that her fiancé was gone and that he wouldn't be coming back. At first, she was in total denial, accusing me of lying to her. Every piece of my heart wished like hell that it was lie. Throwing herself into my arms, she began banging on my chest uncontrollably. Luckily for me, I was so numb that I didn't feel her blows until the next day.

What should have been a celebration had quickly turned into a room full of mourning attendees. Everyone appeared to be in utter disbelief. There wasn't a dry eye in the room as they listened to my sister scream into my chest in heartbroken agony. When I looked up everyone was staring at me as if I were the enemy. In reality, I was just the messenger. And I certainly didn't want to be the one to deliver the news, but I knew I needed to. My sister needed to hear it from me.

"Come on, Babygirl," I whispered, slowly ushering Savonna toward the door. "We need to get over to the hospital."

I wrapped my arm around her waist and led her in the direction of the exit. Unfortunately, she was so distraught that she nearly collapsed to the floor. Thank God, Tim was there to catch her. The two of us worked in tandem to calm her down enough to get her outside and into the back of my car. While Tim climbed into the back seat, holding Savonna as she continued to scream, I sent Sky a text alerting her to the tragic loss of Preston and instructing her to get the family and have everyone meet us at the hospital.

And if the day wasn't bad enough, I had the police called on me while we were sitting in DC traffic, Savonna still screaming in the back seat. Of course, I didn't know that until I was stopped, surrounded on all sides by police cars and officers with guns drawn. At first, I assumed I had run a red light or something, but that didn't warrant the way in which they pulled up on me.

Once I informed the officers of what was going on and that Savonna was my sister, everything worked out in my favor. Apparently, an innocent bystander had heard the screams and thought I was a kidnapper. Luckily for us, the police had heard the call come over the radio so they were familiar with Preston's suicide. I informed them that we were on the way to the hospital but had gotten caught in traffic. Without a second thought, one of the officers offered to give us a police escort to the hospital. Which I gladly accepted.

Savonna's screams were endless, the police not distracting her from what she was feeling inside. The short ride seemed to take an eternity. I felt utterly defeated that there was nothing Tim or I could do to console her. When we arrived a short while later, Tim opened the back door and it was obvious that everything had taken a toll on him. After helping me to pull Savonna from the car, he remained outside while I carried Savonna into the hospital.

As soon as we stepped inside, I rushed Savonna straight back to the emergency department, past Sky and the rest of the family. In my mind, I was bringing her there to see Preston's body so that she would have some kind of concrete closure, but my heart was telling me that it was a bad idea. Regardless, given her state of mind, I knew the hospital was the best place for her. She was so distraught she needed something to calm her down. And that was going to come from the doctors.

When we reached the back a nurse jumped up to stop me until she saw what I was dealing with. Savonna was heaving and coughing so hard that she was having trouble breathing, her body shaking uncontrollably. Ushering us straight into triage, I quickly got Savonna into a seat and pulled the nurse aside so that I could explain what was wrong. The last thing I needed was for her to hear Preston's name and explode all over again.

That was the plan, at least.

Just as I finished explaining what had happened to the nurse, Tootie's voice could be heard shouting at the top of her lungs, "My Son! My Son!"

As soon as Savonna heard her voice, anxiety took over. I truly believe that was the moment reality set in. I watched my sister get up, running in the direction of Tootie's voice. The two of them embraced one another, holding on for dear life. From what I could gather, Tootie was on her way to claim Preston's body, Miles right by her side.

"He's gone, Vonna," Tootie whispered. "He's gone. I don't know how I'm going to make it without him!"

Savonna's head shook from side to side. "No—we're getting married! He's not gone, Tootie. He can't be!" Miles and I exchanged a look, unsure what to do to help either of them. We were just two helpless men watching women that we loved fall apart with no way of consoling them.

I was angry at my loss of control. Looking up at the ceiling with my fists balled, I wished I could punch something. Of course, I knew it wouldn't solve anything. However, with any luck it would replace the pain. If only for a few minutes.

"Tootie, they're waiting on us to claim the body," Miles quietly interjected.

And that's when the real train wreck occurred.

Savonna lost it, shouting, "There isn't a body for her to claim because Preston is waiting for me at the house! He's at home. Safe."

I grabbed Savonna by the arms and pulled her into me while Miles ushered Tootie off in the opposite direction. "Babygirl, I'm here for you," I whispered. "I know it hurts right now, but we're going to get through this." And just like that, I became the villain all over again.

Pounding on my chest, she began kicking and screaming at the top of her lungs. She was so hysterical that nurses came rushing out into the hallway. Sedative in hand, one of the nurses stuck her with the needle while the other two helped get her into a wheelchair before rolling her in a nearby room.

Defeated, I walked out into the waiting area where my family was sitting and let them know what was going on. As expected, I was bombarded with questions about what happened to Preston. Questions I didn't have the answers to myself.

I was mentally exhausted and didn't have the energy to play one hundred questions, but before I could say anything, Cassey stepped in. "Not now, everyone. Please. He's at his peak. Let him have a few moments alone to process everything himself. When he ready, he will answer your questions as best he can."

While I understood and even shared their desire for answers, I knew I wouldn't be able to give them any in my current state. Reluctantly, they all took their seats and we waited until the doctor came out to let us all know that Savonna was okay.

*****

"Samir, you're no longer watching TV, this TV is watching you. We need to talk," Cassey said, taking the remote from my hand and turning off the television.

"What's up?" The last thing I wanted to do was talk, but I knew I had little choice in the matter. *Please, I hope she's not going to nag me.*

"Bae, you need to go talk to a professional. Sitting around here staring at these four walls is not doing anything for your depression," Cassey muttered softly as she climbed into my lap.

"Depression? I'm not depressed!" I shouted in irritation. "I'm just going through something! Can't you understand that" *Oh, so now Cassey wants to play doctor and attempt to diagnose me.* I knew she meant well, but that didn't do anything for the fire raging inside of me.

"Yes, you are going through something! It's called depression. I miss you. The kids miss you. Hell, the kitchen misses you. And you've been right here with us the entire time. Each day is the same. You wake up and then come sit on this couch. As your wife, I'm only going to be so patient. And you damn well the kids don't have any," Cassey said, kissing me on the forehead.

Her words struck me like a blow to the stomach. *If I can't beat this on my own, I might have to force myself to talk to a stranger for my family's sake. Something that I'm normally against. In the meantime, I'm going to put my best foot forward and try to beat it on my own.*

"I apologize that it's taken me a minute to come around. I promise, I'm going to do better."

CHAPTER 6

SKY

"How is she doing today? You look stressed!" Serenity asked as she handed me Lil Sky. I decided to stop by since my life seemed like it was tied up and I didn't get to spend as much time with her as I would have liked.

"Your sister is completely draining me! She refuses to go to the house because she can't bring herself to look at the garage. She refuses to leave her condo, never mind the fact that it's already been sold and no longer belongs to her anymore. Thankfully, after hearing the circumstances, the new owners gave her an extra month. The problem is that Savonna unpacked everything like she doesn't have to move." I sighed, exhausted and frustrated with my sister. I was trying to be as sympathetic as I can but at some point, she has to make a move. I understand what she experienced has caused her unimaginable pain, but she was being so unreasonable.

"Sky, I understand what you're saying, but put yourself in her shoes. I, for one, wouldn't want to move into that house either. Whether she physically saw him hanging there or not, she knows that's the last place he was. That's hard. Perhaps she could sell it and move in with you for the time being?" Serenity suggested, hitting nail on the head.

I knew that was what had to happen. The house needed to be put back on the market and she needed to stay with me until she could stand on her own again. It was the only option she had. I knew I was going to be in for a fight, but what other choice did she really have? She wouldn't stay at the new house and she couldn't stay at the old house. There was no other option.

"You do think sometimes," I joked while playing with the baby. "That's a good idea!" I missed my chubby cheeks more than I missed my own grandchild who I hadn't been able to see since Prince and the hoodrat had been going at it. John and I told Prince so many times to take her to court for visitation. Still, he did nothing. We'll hold his hand all day long, but we're not going to do all the leg work for him. He's a father and it was time he started acting like one.

"Whatever," Serenity rolled her eyes. "I always think. It's not my problem that you never ask the expert in the family. Which you know is me!" she said, pointing at herself with a wide smile on her face.

Oh, how I wish that were true, I thought. Sadly, we all knew just how warped Serenity's thinking was. Granted, she could usually be logical when it came down to other people's lives. Just never her own.

"Have you talked to Samir lately?" I asked. I knew their relationship had been a little rocky as of late, but they seemed to be coming together slowly. I can certainly attest to the fact that Serenity had been a much better sister and an even better aunt to the children than she had been in the past.

In a shocking turn of events, we had become the needy ones—always needing her for something. Not financially, because she still wasn't stable in that area. However, I was glad to hear that she was at least maintaining her household. Something that hadn't been done in quite some time.

"I called him the other day. Cassey said he was taking a nap. When he finally called me back, I was giving Sky a bath. We should probably take a ride over there," she suggested, waiting for me to respond.

"I don't know—" I wasn't sure if I should. For my own sanity. Samir wasn't exactly in the best place right now and dealing with two of them in one day—well, I feared it might be bad for my own mental health. It seemed that when I wasn't dealing with Savonna, I was dealing with Samir. Cassey called me six to seven times a day to vent. And that was on the days that I didn't go over there.

"It won't take me long to get the kids together," she assured. "Besides, we need to get out of this house for a little while." Apparently, Serenity's car went up on her again a few weeks ago and they had been confined since then. I'm sure that by now they all had cabin fever.

"Okay, I'll text Cassey and let her know that we're coming over." While Serenity was dealing with the other three kids, I got the baby together. Once everyone was ready to go, we hopped in my car and headed over to Samir's.

*****

When we stepped inside, I got the shock of the century when I saw the two newlyweds, Jacobi and Tamela sitting on the couch. I couldn't be certain, but if I had to guess, this was Jacobi's first time in Samir and Cassey's home. Until now, he'd never come inside based on principle. He couldn't stand Cassey, and since this was just as much her house as it was Samir's, he stayed away. I don't know how much they were interacting before we got there, but when we walked in Tamela and Cassey were chatting it up like old besties. Regardless, I was glad they were here so that I could apologize for not being able to attend their wedding.

"Congrats on the wedding, you two. I'm sorry that I couldn't make it."

"There's no apology necessary," Jacobi said as he stood to give me a hug.

From behind him, I could see Tamela nod in agreement. "Yes, and thank you for the gift. We truly appreciate it."

It wasn't long before I ended up in the kitchen preparing food for everyone. Normally, Samir would have been in the kitchen telling me all the ways in which I was doing things wrong. However, he never came in. Instead, Cassey and Serenity would pop in-between bouts of hollering at the kids. Meanwhile, Tamela hung with me the whole time, holding Lil Sky and keeping her company. I wasn't exactly prepared, so I made a quick meal of burgers, hot dogs, steak, ribs, baked beans, fries, tossed salad, and corn on the cob. I gave them a cook-out without the grill. And boy did I put my foot in it. The kids even came back for seconds; us grown folks were full and tired.

"Jacobi, Tamela—how long is going to be before I get a niece or nephew?" I asked, watching Tamela with Lil Sky in her arms while we were all relaxing in the living room. I have to say, I was impressed how well Lil Sky was doing. She's not exactly the friendliest baby and she only likes who she likes.

"Uhhhhh—I'm still getting used to the fact that I have a wife," Jacobi replied. "For now, I'm good with the godchildren." We all burst out laughing because he wasn't lying. Hell, I still can't believe it myself.

"Well, playing with this bundle of joy has me getting baby fever," Tamela admitted. The words had no sooner left her mouth when Jacobi politely took Lil Sky out of her hands and placed her in the arms of her mama.

Everybody fell out laughing. I was in tears from laughing so hard. *Well, I guess they won't be having any children anytime soon.*

"Come on, y'all, let's play a game of spades," Serenity suggested, knowing damn well we wouldn't play just one game. *This is going to be an all-nighter and I still have to drop her off back home before I can go home myself.*

We decided to do women against the men. First up, the married couples. Cassey and Tamela played against Jacobi and Samir. As expected, the husbands tore up the wives. Serenity and I were next, playing against the winners, Jacobi and Samir, who were talking mad shit. They kept telling us to sit down so that we could get our butts whooped.

Of course, we shut them two sore losers up and they ended up getting set on the first hand, which automatically qualified Serenity and I for the win. While we beat the brakes off of Cassey and Tamela, the boys sat quietly waiting their next turn so that they could attempt to redeem themselves.

It's funny how quickly the tables can turn. Difference is, Serenity and I backed up all the shit we were talking, pulling a Boston on the two sore losers. Before I knew it, we were in the midst of an all-out spades war. Five games later, and Serenity and I were still winning.

"Does anybody have any idea what time it is?" Cassey asked, obviously tired of losing. "And who the hell is getting up with these kids?" We all looked at the clock and was surprised to find that it was four in the morning.

"Oh, my goodness!" I immediately checked my phone to see if John had tried to reach me. Luckily, he hadn't. I could only assume he was asleep.

"Well, Samir, Cassey, do y'all mind if I just crash here rather than waking up the kids?" Serenity asked.

"That's fine. I wouldn't want you to wake them up at this hour. Besides, we've got a spare bedroom that never gets used," Cassey suggested, looking over at Samir to make sure it was okay.

"That's fine. And I'll get up with the kids. You two can sleep in late." I loved Samir. He was always so considerate, letting the mommy's get some rest.

With Serenity and the kids taken care of, Jacobi, Tamela and I said our goodbyes and headed out the door. As late as it is, you would have thought that we all would have been tired long before now. I guess it's true what they say, 'Time flies when you're having fun.' But after everything that had happened, I knew this was exactly what Samir needed: good food, good company, and lots of laughter.

Cassie said things have been different since Samir found Preston, but I didn't know the full scope of it until he was a no show in the kitchen. Beneath the fake façade, I could tell Samir wasn't himself. He hated Cassey even being in the kitchen, especially while he was home. That was his domain. Yet, despite that fact, he remained in the living room with Jacobi. He didn't even peek in to aggravate me like he usually did.

*****

By the time I arrived home, I was completely exhausted. I couldn't even remember the last time I'd hung out so late. Though what was most surprising was the fact that John didn't even try to call me. Anything could have happened to me and he wouldn't even know.

I stepped inside and found the house was quiet, just like I expected. Quietly, I crept into the bedroom and ditched my clothes, leaving only my bra and panties on. Trying not to wake John, I carefully slid into bed.

"It's five in the fucking morning and you come sliding in here like shit is gravy! Where the hell have you been?" John shouted, startling me.

"Who the hell do you think you are, talking to me like that?" I snapped. There was no way in hell he was going to come at me like I was out in them streets whoring around. "Not that I owe you an explanation, but I was over Samir's playing cards. And if you were so concerned, why the hell didn't you call me to find out where I was?"

"I shouldn't have to call my wife! My wife should come in here at a decent hour because she has a husband at home!" I could already see where this was going. John was just looking for a fight and I was too tired and it was too early. This wasn't something that I normally did, so I didn't know why he was making such a big deal out of it.

"I lost track of time. Besides, this was good for Samir. He's been having a hard time lately and we were trying to snap him out of it." Without another word, I rolled over and turned my back to him.

"Samir, Savonna and Serenity—that's all you ever care about! For years I've played second, third, fourth. I'm always on the back burner. You never put me first! Not once. This family, our family, should be your first priority! Not that you would care to notice, but my family has stuff going on too. Have you ever seen me kick you to the side for my family issues? No! I'm fucking tired of it! You're never here, always running behind one of them!" John jumped out of bed and started putting his clothes on.

"Where are you going this early in the morning?" I asked, knowing John was just picking an argument. Everything between us had been fine, so I didn't understand why he was acting like this. It just came out of nowhere.

"After everything I just said, that's what ask me? You don't get it, Sky! Why does it matter where I'm going? It's obvious you don't really care. Have you ever heard of taking care of your own home first before you go cleaning up somebody else's shit?"

He better take his ass in that garage to smoke his weed so he can calm down and I can get some sleep before I come out this bed. For all of this, I might as well have just stayed at Samir's house. I'm hanging out with family and he's over here acting like I abandoned him with babies to take care of.

"John, ple—"

"John, please, my ass! You bend over backwards for everyone except me. This is it, Sky. I'm done. Either I become a priority in your life or I'm walking away from this marriage. You can have everything; I don't give a damn. Either way, you need to decide. And I mean today, not tomorrow!"

I know damn well he's not being this selfish, I thought in disbelief. *Of course, things aren't normal in my life right now. We all suffered a tragedy. And it's because of that I have to help my brother and sister. They're the ones who need me right now. Not John. He can wait!*

Chapter 7

Serenity

Well, I am once again a married woman. Iron and I finally tied the knot. Since Gary had the kids for the weekend and Sky had the baby, I was finally able to make it happen. It's a little crazy that my husband is doing time for a crime that he committed on me. But I truly believe things had to fall apart in order to bring us together. Now, I just needed to figure out how I was going to break the news to my family.

Trust me when I tell you that I am in no rush to become the black sheep again. Especially now that I was on good terms with all of them, including Mom and Dad. Telling them that I married the man that put me in the hospital while pregnant with his baby—that would ruin everything. But that's a bridge that I'll have to cross when the time comes. For now, I intend to enjoy my time with my family. While I still have it.

The minute my car got fixed, I sent in my marriage packet and fees. Since this was my second jail wedding I was very familiar with how the process worked. I had gotten our marriage license a couple of months ago–luckily, they don't expire in D.C. because sometimes it could take more than thirty days–so all I had to do was go through the list of approved pastors and pick one.

As luck would have it, I managed to get ahold of the first one and Pastor Anderson agreed to officiate our ceremony. Which left us with one dilemma: who was going to be our witness? That was the one time I wished I'd had at least one female friend. But I didn't. The sad reality is that if weren't family, you didn't stand a chance with me. I'd been like that all of my life. Because I didn't have anyone that I trusted enough to call, Iron chose Bubba, his cellmate, to be the witness. Once we had all that in place, it was time to plan.

Knowing the date was coming up soon, I got to work looking for a dress. I wasn't looking for fancy, only sexy. It didn't take me long to locate a nice one online, which I promptly ordered with hopes that it would fit. When ordering online, you never really know what you're going to get. Sometimes it was a hit and sometimes it was an utter disaster. Luckily for me, this one happened to be a hit. The dress fit snuggly, highlighting all of my curves, which I hoped would entice Iron.

The moment he laid eyes on me, he lit up. We may not have been able to make love that day, but I knew he would damn sure be fantasizing about it that night. While to many it may not have seemed like a lot, but Iron and I, it was just as amazing as any big lavish wedding you would see on TV.

*****

I felt like I was floating on cloud nine. I was officially the wife of Mr. Tyquan Smith, or as I referred to him, Iron. My second go with marriage and his first. My life had never felt so complete. Even when I was married to Gary, something always felt off. Sure, I loved him. But at the time, it was more of the right thing to do. After all, he was the father of my child. With Iron, everything is different. Unlike my marriage to Gary, I felt like what Iron and I had was fate. I wasn't forced or pressured to forgive him. It just happened.

I still get chills when I think about how everything happened. *My God is so amazing. What the devil meant for bad, He turned it all around for my own good. When my husband comes home, everyone will finally see that he's not the same man. They will be believers just like me.*

It's hard holding in good news, but I also knew that good news to me, would not necessarily be looked at the same by everybody else. Especially when it came to my family.

Savonna damn sure didn't want to hear the word *love*. She's mean and downright negative—almost unbearable to be around. Understandable given everything she had been through. Even after all these months, she hadn't come to grips that Preston was gone and he wasn't coming back. In my opinion, she needed to try and move forward. And I'm not talking about finding another man. To be honest, I'm not sure she'll ever be ready for that. But she needs to go back to work and get out of the house for a little while.

Then there's Sky. Ever since John finally decided to become a man and leave her, she'd been salty. Deep down, I don't think she believed he would ever do it. In the blink of any eye her fake, perfect world imploded. And now everyone knew that her *perfect* life wasn't all that perfect after all. Unfortunately for her, she didn't have much say that. After their split, John had been quite vocal in letting everyone know of their separation. It seemed the only two holding it together were Samir and Cassey. And I wouldn't dare tell either one of them.

Cassey and I had never really been close but recently, our relationship was blooming. I respected her for holding Samir down while he was dealing with his depression. While that's exactly what she's supposed to do as his wife, many wouldn't. Cassey stuck by him and called out his bullshit while carefully molding him out of his depression. It wasn't easy for, her but I could see he was making progress and slowly coming back. She was his ride or die forreal.

After Preston's death, I'd been over there visiting and he was just lying about the house while Cassey handled everything else. Samir Jr appeared to be having a difficult time adjusting to his father's new behavioral pattern and had been taking it out on Cassey, running that smart mouth of his. You ask me, Cassey needs to knock a few of his teeth out. He'll stop testing her then.

Samir and Jr have always had a special relationship, one that only a father and son could understand. But lately, Samir hasn't been paying him any attention. It's easy for me to recognize the signs because Quavon did me the same way when Gary was in and out of jail. I had to tear him a new one a couple of times for undermining my authority. I told them all time and time again that the one thing I wouldn't do was deal with disrespectful children. I'd sooner knock them into next week. When it comes to me, it damn well better be 'yes, Ma'am' and 'no, Ma'am'. What I say goes, no exceptions. Quavon and Quinton are almost teenagers now, and much bigger than me, but they know better than to try me. Which is precisely how Cassey needs to handle my nephew.

When I'm around, he acts like he's actually got some sense. I suppose it's because all the kids know that I'm the aunt that will beat their asses in front of their parents. And their Aunt Sky was no different. More than likely why we're not the favorites. When my nephews would jump out of line, she was the first one to jump in their asses.

Savonna—she's the fun aunt. She'd never put her hands on any of them, but she also doesn't have to. When they're with her, it's all about having a good time. When my kids were growing up, I would sometimes use the 'You're not going with your Aunt Savonna if you don't do what I tell you.' They always did.

I hate to say it, but it appeared all the kids were losing respect for her. For the past couple of years, she'd been in and out of their lives. When she went through something, everything around her came to a halt. It wasn't fair to them. Kids don't understand that you're hurting. All they wanted to know was why she wasn't coming to pick them up. I'm just happy she doesn't have her own children. I could only imagine what things would be like then. When you have children, there is no such thing as putting them on the back burner.

The sad truth is that Savonna needed to learn that no matter what was going on in her life, she had to move forward.

I stepped up to the plate as much as I can afford, but I couldn't do the things that she would do for them. Once a month I would try to take them for a picnic in the park or go roller skating. This month, I decided to take them to the movies. I knew it would cut into my bill money, but that was a sacrifice I was willing to make. I figured as long as I put something on my bills, I would be okay. I could only hope that one day, my finances would change and it wouldn't hurt me to do anything for, or with, them. Until then, I would scrape together whatever I could to make sure the kids were all taken care of.

*****

"Hello?" I answered as I picked up the phone.

"Hi," Miles greeted, his voice soft. "I just needed to hear a familiar voice." It was always nice when I got to talk to Miles. Ever since Preston's repass, we'd kept in touch with one another. We had a connection. While we were both misunderstood, we understood each other perfectly.

"Is it safe to say that you're having a bad day?" Of course, I knew the answer without him saying a word. It was the only time we really leaned on each other, which I had no problem with. And neither did he. While other people got offended if you only called them when you had a problem, Miles and I embraced it.

"You already know," he choked. "No matter how much I try to block out that vision, it still surfaces. Every time I close my eyes, I see Preston hanging in that garage." I listened to his ragged breathing as he tried to work out what he wanted to say.

"How did you get past a man shooting you and forcing your children to watch as he sexually abused you?" My whole body clenched as the words exited his mouth. And not in a good way.

While I had been taught to forgive and not harbor any ill feelings toward others who may have done me wrong, my children didn't have that same teaching instilled in them. Back when I was growing up, we forgave too much. Many of whom didn't deserve it. The last thing I ever wanted was for my children to forgive people who took advantage of them with little to no concern for their feelings.

They were better than that.

I was better than that.

"I don't think that we can compare the two. Love is what helped me to forgive. I know that it sounds crazy—I can't even comprehend it—but trust me when I say that God truly does work in mysterious ways." I've been asked a number of times how I was able to forgive Iron for everything he'd done to me and my children, and I don't honestly think I'll ever be able to give anyone a concrete answer. Deep down, I know I should hate the man. But I don't. The only explanation I have that makes any sense at all is that it had to be the Lord.

"I keep praying about it, like you told me to do, but my mind refuses to rest. Every now and again, I find I'm blaming myself. Like I should have seen the warning signs. I just wish I could have that day back to do things differently. Maybe I could have saved him."

While our situations weren't the same, I understand where he was coming from. However, he needed to stop blaming himself because he did nothing wrong. Sadly, guilt is a fickle thing. While you may know in your heart of hearts that you have no reason to feel guilty, it can still eat you up from the inside out.

"Miles! Cut it out!" I scolded, my voice firm. "There is absolutely nothing that you could have done to keep Preston from killing himself. He suffered from depression—more severely than any of us could have ever imagined. That's not on you!"

"I know. But—"

"No!" I stated firmly, cutting him off. "This is what I want you to do. When you say your prayers tonight, I want you to ask God to give you clarity and peace over Preston's passing. Ask him to remove all doubt and blame that you are carrying." If my parents taught me nothing else, they taught me the power of prayer.

"Serenity, I've never been a religious or spiritual man. I wasn't raised up in the church and there was certainly no Bible lying around my house. But I'm also not ignorant. Do you think there's any possible way that Preston went to H–Heaven?" he stammered. I was really hoping that Miles wasn't hinting at this question because I didn't want to be the one to answer it. While I wanted to say yes to ease his mind, the scripture tells us that he's burning up in Hell.

"Miles, I can't answer that. You will have to seek your own knowledge and wait for God to give you an answer." That's the best way that I knew to answer his question without completely destroying him.

"Well, can you pray for me like you usually do?" he asked, his voice barely above a whisper. Little did he know, I kept him in my prayers.

Miles was the type of man that needed answers and closure before he could move on. Which was why he was still caught up on his ex leaving him. While I felt bad for him, I loved the fact that he could tap into the spiritual side of me. The side that most weren't even aware existed. Yet, despite the fact that he wasn't raised in a religious or spiritual home, he did. Some days, completely out of the blue, he'd shoot me a text and ask me to pray for him. While he was so far away from me, he always felt so close.

"Let us pray. Lord, we come to you today asking for forgiveness for our sins, known and unknown. Father God, we give you all the glory. For you are worthy to be praised. Father, I come to you today interceding on Miles' behalf. God, the troubles that this man is facing—only you can fix. His heart is troubled in ways only you can mend. Father, I don't have the answers that he's looking for. But you do! Lord, I'm asking that you give Miles the peace that surpasses all understanding. I'm also asking that you give him the strength to trust you through his process. Father, his faith is weary, for he does not know you like I do. I ask that you come into his life, Lord. Show yourself to him in a way that only he will know and will leave little doubt of who it is. Let your Angels hover over him and protect him from every unholy attack that the Devil has set forth in his path. In his weakness, Lord, I ask that you strengthen him. Through you, God, let Miles get the victory! In Jesus' name we pray, Amen!"

"Amen. Thank you, Serenity. I really needed that." Miles' voice was muffled, as if he were crying on the other end of the phone. I knew that meant the spirit was moving within him.

"You're welcome, anytime." My mother always taught me that when someone needed prayer, you pray for them. It costs zero dollars to intercede on someone's behalf and that's when the Lord blesses you. And Heaven knows, I needed all of my blessings.

"I'm going to be making a trip soon. I feel like I need to see you," he said. Miles had been talking about coming back to see me for months. I'll admit, I needed something to look forward to and seeing him would do just that.

"It would be nice to be in some good company. Lord knows I need it. Just give me a heads up so that I can make arrangements." This *friendship* was something different for me because I'd never really had any friends. It had always been just me and my family. I wasn't even close to my in-laws.

"I will keep you apprised of the situation. It will most likely be in the next couple of weeks. And don't worry about getting a babysitter. I'm kid friendly." Miles laughed. It was like music to my ears given the way our conversations first began. He sounded so defeated, broken.

"Well, I'm not. I'm stuck with these kids twenty-four seven. I need some time to myself in the company of adults. Which means I'll definitely be getting a babysitter, Sir!" We were both cracking up as we said our goodbyes.

CHAPTER 8

SAVONNA

"Savonna! Vonna! Savonna!" I could hear Tootie calling my name but I couldn't respond. It felt like my body was stuck, paralyzed.

"Y–Yes!" I shouted, forcing myself to speak as I stared out the window with tears streaming down my face while thinking about Preston, like I usually did! One minute, I was angry. The next, I was overcome with sadness.

"It's time, Honey," Tootie whispered as she placed her hand in mine.

"Time? Time for what?" I asked in confusion, never turning to face her.

"Time for you to try and move on with your life. You need to get back to work and do all the things that Preston would have wanted you to do."

Now she's starting to sound like everyone else. Since when is there a time limit on grieving? I'll take as much time as I damn well please. Nobody will rush me. Not ever! I thought in anger.

"I wish everyone would realize that I'm on my own time, not theirs!" I snapped, trying to be as respectful as I could. For the life of me, I couldn't figure out why Tootie was acting like life just went on after losing her only son. She should be slumped over somewhere, grieving for her child. Instead, she bounced back like it happened five years ago.

"Savonna, look at me!" Tootie yelled.

"What?" I shouted as I turned to face her.

"It's time to end your pity party, get off your ass and do something! Preston is never coming back! So, if you're waiting for some kind of miracle healing, it's never going to happen. This is your new reality and you have to learn to live in it. It isn't just some break up. You didn't just wake up one day and no longer want him. He's dead and he's never coming back!" Without another word, Tootie stormed out of the house.

It's crazy how everyone believes they're an expert on my grieving process. Trying to tell me how to heal and what they think I should be doing. While their lives went on like nothing happened, mine stopped completely. I can't relate to these people and they certainly can't relate to me. In the blink of an eye, I'd lost the love of my life, my future husband. I needed time to grieve in my own way. Even after all this time, I still woke up every morning looking for him, waiting to feel his soft lips on my cheeks. I'd do anything to hear his voice whisper, *'Good Morning, Baby.'*

But if you ask *the experts*, they'll tell you that I'm milking the clock. What they don't understand is just how broken my heart is. They don't feel the pain that I suffer on a daily basis, the panic attacks. So, the question becomes, who are these people to tell me how to grieve? As far as I'm concerned, they're all strangers.

I thought staying here with Tootie would give me comfort–and it did at first. We'd stay up half the night talking and crying together. Now—now she doesn't want any part of–what she calls–harping on Preston. Me, I call it expressing myself while trying to keep his spirit alive. While I was still grieving the loss of the man I loved, she was running around here living her best life. Looking at her, you would never know that her son was dead. I just couldn't figure out how she got up every day and went out.

One day, I asked her if we could dedicate one day a week to Preston? Would you believe that woman flat out told me NO? According to her, I did that enough for the both of us. That was the moment I realized that I was alone in my grief.

At times, I wished there were a way for them to wear my heart for a day. I can guarantee they would throw it right back at me and never utter another word about how they think my life should be progressing. And if that weren't enough, I was growing quite tired of being asked when I was going back to work. *"Don't you think it's time you go back to work?" "Don't you think going back to work will help you take your mind off of it?"* Who in their right damn mind would think I would want to rush back to the very place I got the news that my fiancé was dead? During my bridal shower, no less.

Think, people. Think!

Truth is, I don't know if I'll ever go back to work. The only thing that would accomplish is bringing about even more pain. For the time being, I didn't care to ever practice law again. But once again, according to all the experts on grief, work is precisely what I need. They can't seem to understand that what I need is Preston. I need him back in my arms with memories of our dream wedding and perfect home that I picked out for the two of us. What I need is to be feeling another life growing inside of me—a child born of true love. What I need is to be full of joy, like I once was. What I need—what is need are some damn answers as to why the love of my life would just up and kill himself and leave me broken.

Unfortunately, everything that I needed, I couldn't have! It was all gone, everything I'd longed for is gone. My entire life was now utterly meaningless.

For as long as I live, I'll never forget Preston's last words to me. *"I love you, Savonna. Have a great day!"*

*****

I woke up that morning like I usually did, greeted by his soft lips peppering kisses across my cheek. "Good morning, my gorgeous wife to be." Just hearing the word wife, made me quiver. But it wasn't the word itself, it was the way in which he said it. His voice held a special tone that always turned me on.

Clenching my thighs together, I desperately wanted to stay in bed and make love like we would often do. As if reading my mind, Preston laughed and said, "No, Baby, I don't want you to be late for work! Besides, you wore me out last night!" I was both shocked and disappointed because Preston had never told me no.

I crossed my arms and pouted like one of my nieces and nephews when they didn't get their way. Another chuckle escaped him. "Baby, that won't work today! I have a lot of work to do and my wife-to-be is very demanding. If I don't have the rest of this stuff moved into this house today she's going to be pouting forreal!"

I unfolded my arms and pulled Preston on top of me. "Just a quickie and I'll give you a pass for today!" We both knew that if we did this, we would be tangled in the sheets for no less than thirty minutes as Preston was never good at quickies. He just couldn't do it. For him, it was always all or nothing. And today was going to be no different.

Preston jumped out of bed like he was on fire and pointed his finger at me accusingly. "You are something else, my love. Always determined to have it your way. All because you know it's hard for me to resist you."

Without a word, Preston sauntered into the kitchen to make my tea while I laid in bed angry as hell with wet ass. When he walked back in the room with my tea, I sat up with my attitude on a thousand. He spoiled me rotten and I wanted that to continue on until forever. "Don't you dare start anything that you can't commit to, Preston. I have a problem with people switching up on me at the last minute." I sipped my tea.

Preston took the cup out of my hand and placed it on the nightstand. Taking both of my hands in his, he said, "Savonna stop it! Get yourself together! You will not always get a yes from me.

Just like I won't always get one from you. That's just how life is. Now, get up and get ready for work. I don't want you to be late!"

*****

Looking back, that should have been my clue that something was up. I had nothing special going on. It was just a regular day at the office. Yet, for some reason, he was insistent that I not be late. Something he had never done before.

As I climbed out of bed, I remember thinking, *Why is he making such a big stink about me getting to work on time?* It wouldn't be until much later that I found out why.

*****

Hurrying into the bathroom, I took my shower and got ready for work. Still, I was a bit bothered by everything that had occurred earlier. When I stepped into the kitchen a short while later, Preston was finishing up breakfast. He had made my favorite because he knew how much I loved his pancakes.

"Here, Greedy, my famous pancakes and some scrambled eggs with cheese and sausage. Also, you look very nice." I couldn't help the smile that crossed my face.

"Thank you, Baby. I so appreciate you," I said, kissing his lips before turning to brush my ass up against him, reminding him of what he'd missed out on. "Oh, now you're trying to be funny?" We both laughed.

While eating breakfast together we discussed our plans for the day. He had started his vacation time and this was my last day at work since we both had a ton to do before the wedding. However, the most important thing was making sure that we were moved into our new home. Luckily, his best friend, Miles, was flying in to help and would be staying until after the wedding.

I could tell Preston was excited to see his best friend. And after everything I'd heard about him, I couldn't wait to meet the infamous Miles myself. The closeness the two men seemed to share reminded me so much of Samir and Jacobi. The way they would talk and laugh on the phone for hours at a time—it just came so naturally. The two men were so close that Miles had already been named Godfather to our unborn children. Preston and I had even agreed that after we came back from the honeymoon, our first trip together would be to fly out to see Miles for a long weekend.

Preston told me everything he had planned for the day. It was all worked out. Apparently, he, Miles, and Samir were planning to meet up a bit later in the afternoon. He was going to have them help him move the remaining items to the house. Everything sounded great, so I left it in his capable hands. As for me, I had a meeting with our wedding coordinator and an appointment at the bakery to look at the cake. Afterward, I assured Preston that we would touch base and meet up for dinner.

When he had finished dinner, I gathered my things and Preston walked me to my car where we exchanged a kiss and said our I love you's. I climbed inside and started up the car. "I love you, Savonna. Have a great day!" he said again as I blew him a kiss and pulled off.

*****

When I got to work, the entire office was decorated and a giant banner hung on the wall that read: **CONGRATULATIONS, SAVONNA!**

Balloons flooded the office with a bunch of gifts sitting on a nearby table. I had no clue they had anything planned, but now I knew why Preston was so insistent that I arrive on time. As it turned out, today wasn't going to be a work day at all, it was a day of celebration.

Everyone stood, wide smiles upon their faces as the tears welled in my eyes. They didn't have to do anything for my wedding, but they did it because they cared. I was completely shocked. They had really outdone themselves. "If you will excuse me a moment, I need to text my fiancé and yell at him for his deceitfulness," I told everyone with a chuckle.

SAVONNA: You could have just told me! 😠

PRESTON: No, I couldn't. 😊 🤍

That was the last time we spoke. *And people wonder why I'm so fucked up,* I inwardly groaned. I'd be a rich woman if I had a dollar for the number of times people have said, *"There had to be some kind of sign. Perhaps you missed something. Or maybe he got cold feet."*

They were wrong.

There were never any signs of depression, only happiness. Preston wanted to marry me. I didn't have to pressure him into asking me, it was all of his own doing! I didn't have to tell him to get close to my brother. As a matter of fact, I was completely against it! Yet, despite my protests, he pushed his way into my life and everybody fell in love with him. I just couldn't understand why a man who was so deeply in love with me would do something like this. In the end, it all came down to one thing.

Preston didn't love me.

How could he have possibly loved me when he didn't even love himself?

'Oh, Savonna, I love you more than life itself.'

'Oh, Savonna, my life means nothing if you're not in it.'

'Savonna, I intend to give you the world!'

It was all lies. I should have known better because the only thing men are good for is hurting me. It's like I'm a magnet for pain. *How pathetic I must be to even think that a man could actually love me! I* mentally chastised. *I'm never enough. I'm never gonna be enough! I'm always the one left picking up the remains. Shit! It's called shit! And shit stinks! I have to get it through my head once and for all that love don't love me! Never has, never will!*

I'm done!

CHAPTER 9

SAMIR

Since Preston's death I'd been fighting this demon called depression. Slowly but surely, I was pulling myself back up. After Cassey's ultimatum that I see a therapist or I shake off the funk myself, I had working hard to pull myself out of the darkness. A therapist was my last option. Especially since I'm just not much of a believer. My belief is that leaning on the word of God and praying daily will bring me out of anything.

Although given my recent bout of depression, I can see why we have such an unmanaged drug epidemic. Everybody is trying to escape this crazy cruel world we live in. If I'm this shook behind seeing Preston's lifeless body hanging from his garage, I can only imagine what these young cats in the streets go·through when they see their friends getting shot up. They all play that hard shit, but I know their insides have to be torn up. Their young minds aren't equipped to deal with the horrors of everyday life.

And people wonder why the world is so crazy.

There are plenty of days and nights that I just wanted a hit or pill—something to take the edge off. The difference is that I know better. I was raised to seek the Lord in times of trouble. Young men these days aren't being raised the same way I was. They aren't being taught scripture. Instead, the streets are their teacher.

My wake-up call, which showed me how far I had fallen, came when Cassey was in the kitchen cooking dinner. I was laying on the couch, which had become my temporary bedroom thanks to the many sleepless nights I'd had. Some nights, I would wake up crying, completely distraught. So, in an effort to hide my weakness from the rest of my family, I opted to sleep on the couch. Anyways, from where I was lying, I could hear Samir Jr talking back, as if he were suddenly the man of the house. From what I could make out, he was refusing to eat the chicken his mother had prepared and told her she better go to McDonald's and get him something else. I laid there listening for a little while to see if Cassey was gonna smack him clear across the mouth, but it never happened. Instead, she battled back and forth with a child.

Who's the parent in this situation? I thought in irritation. Still, it wasn't enough to make me get up from where I was laying.

"Boy, you better chill out before I tell your father about that mouth of yours!"

Samir Jr scoffed. "Go tell him. I don't give a damn. He ain't gonna do nothing to me."

That was the day that I realized just how absent I'd been. I was in the house but I wasn't really in the house. Normally, anytime Cassey would threaten to me about their attitudes, both kids would straighten up. It was obvious that my presence was no longer enough. I needed to be involved.

While I was wallowing in my depression, my son was losing all respect for me and my daughter was becoming just as sassy as she wanted to be. I would not allow that to happen on my watch. Determined not to become my brother-in-law, John, I bolted up from the couch and walked into the kitchen.

"Who in the hell do you think you're talking to?" I asked, my voice raised. Jr frowned, mean mugging me, but he also didn't answer. I snatched him up and dragged his little ass into the nearby bathroom. "I'm gonna ask you again—who were you talking to like that?" That time I could see a little bit of fear coming from him, but he still refused to answer me.

Losing my patience, I grabbed him by the neck and lifted him off the ground, dangling him in the air. "Now answer me! Who in the hell were you talking like that to?"

"Mommy, he choked, fear filling his eyes.

"What does the word disrespectful mean?"

"Talking back to an adult and not being nice, he replied.

"Okay, as long as you know!" Without another word, I went to whooping his disrespectful little ass. After I had finished beating his ass, I informed him that he was on an extended punishment. Which he knew meant until I said otherwise.

Very rarely did I ever have to put my hands on my kids. For the most part, they always listened. My children knew they had really messed up when I reached that point. Now, Cassey might have to smack them here and there, but that seemed to be the norm for most women.

As of late, he'd been acting like the good son that I raised him to be. Now, it still remains to be seen if the lesson had actually been learned. Only time would tell. Cassey and her soft ass kept asking if he could just watch a little TV, but my answer continued to be no. The only thing he was allowed to do was go to school and come home. If he needed entertainment, he could read a damn book. Maybe he would learn something about treating his parents right.

Kids these days thought they could say whatever they wanted and get away with it, which was something I never would have done to my own parents. I knew better. While other parents may allow their kids to talk to them any way they wanted, mine would respect their mother and I. The minute they didn't was the minute they would find somewhere else to lay their heads. You let it slide once and it was guaranteed to happen again. While I was certain that wasn't the first time Jr got out of control, it was the first time that I wasn't so out of it that I couldn't deal with it.

*****

"Hey, Babe, how are you feeling?" Cassey asked as she walked in with bags from the grocery store. It annoyed the hell out of me. If I was home, I would always carry the bags in for her and she knew it. All she had to do was call or honk the horn.

"I'm good. Are there any more bags in the car?" I asked, taking the bags from her hands and carrying them into the kitchen.

"Just a couple," Cassey nodded.

"Jr, go get the rest of the bags out of your mother's car!" I yelled upstairs. As expected, he didn't take any time getting down the stairs and out the door. Jr. had been trying his best to stay on my good side. Not being able to go outside was damn near killing him.

"I got something new on the menu!" Cassey said excitedly. "I'm going to try making some eggplant for dinner." *Oh, Lord, the kids are going to starve to death and so am I if it isn't good*, I thought to myself. Normally, I wouldn't even let her in the kitchen, but Cassey had been putting her foot down while I was on my hiatus. And while I was back, I couldn't bring myself to try and force her out.

"Sounds good. Those two little ones have never had it, so do you have a backup dish for them?"

Back in the day, when I was growing up, you had to eat whatever was cooked. Whether you liked it or not. I remember a number of times that I was forced to eat liver and onions. It was the most disgusting, vile thing I'd ever eaten. It's one of those things you have to have an acquired taste to eat. As a matter of principle, I didn't subject my kids to that same upbringing. If they don't like what's cooked, they get to eat something else. I can't even begin to tell you how many times I went to bed hungry, sneaking into the kitchen and burying my food in the trash.

"Cereal," she stated matter of fact. "They'll love that! I don't feel like making two meals tonight." I watched as she put the groceries away, pulling out everything she needed to prepare dinner.

"I love you, Cassey." I'm not normally the mushy type, but I felt it was important for her to hear me say it. Lately, I found myself saying it more and more to her, the kids, my sister's and parents. If something were to ever happen to me, I wanted them to know that I loved them. After all, tomorrow is not promised to any of us.

"Aww, Babe—I love you, too! I'm so glad that you're back. You had me worried for a minute there. I've noticed that you've been more attentive than you've have been. I kinda like it." Cassey placed a chaste kiss to my lips and held onto me for dear life.

"You can thank Preston. He did this. His death gave me a whole new perspective on life. You just never know when it's your time to come home." Cassey and I embraced one another for a long minute, no words needing to be exchanged. The silence between us said more than any actual words ever could have.

The death of either one of us—having to live without the other––it would be unbearable.

"I better get to cooking before y'all's stomachs start growling," Cassey muttered before getting to work on our meal. Standing in the doorway of kitchen, I watched in admiration. I was normally very critical when it came to food, but I forced myself to remain silent while watching her move about the kitchen. I had to admit, she was doing pretty good.

For the first time in a long time, my wife and I were actually enjoying each other's company. We shared quality time in the kitchen, talking, laughing, and joking. We were like two kids trying to catch up after returning from a long summer break. It was certainly a far cry from the distant, uninvolved man I had become after Preston's death. And not just from my wife and kids—from everyone.

I had missed so much while I was lost in sea of my depression. Luckily for me, Cassie was current on the latest news. I felt horrible that I'd left my entire family to deal with their own heartbreak when they needed me most. Especially after Cassie told me all the latest.

Apparently, John ended up leaving Sky. While I knew they'd had problems in the past, I didn't think he'd ever have the balls to leave her. I hope, for their sake, they work it out. Savonna, still completely heartbroken, had finally moved out of Tootie's. While I understand why she was staying there, it was well overdue.

How did I let myself get so deep into my own depression that I wasn't aware of what was happening in my own family? I mentally chastised. *I can't do that to them again. I can't do that to myself again.* My ignorance on the subject made me believe that only women suffered from depression. *Perhaps that's why it hit me. It was a life lesson so that I could wise up.*

When she had finished, Cassie made a plate for each of us and we sat down as a family at the table to eat dinner together like we used to do. And as it turned out, Cassie and I were both correct when it came to the kids. They weren't trying to hear about eating no eggplant, but they were perfectly happy to be eating cereal. While we enjoyed our dinner, I asked the kids what was going on in school and we shared a few laughs together.

I'd become so lost in the depths of my depression that I nearly forgot what it felt like to laugh. Thankfully, our kids had quite the sense of humor. They started mimicking their teachers before eventually moving onto us. Amani had Cassey down to a T and Jr. had perfected me. The two of them roleplayed us so well, that Cassey and I were in tears from laughing so hard. It was such a relief, like a weight had been lifted.

After dinner, I dismissed the little lady and the woman of the house to go enjoy themselves while Jr and I cleaned up the kitchen and put the food away. It was time he learned that kitchen work wasn't just a woman's job as he has so incorrectly assumed up to this point. I informed him that there was no such thing as man's job or a woman's job when it came to maintaining a home. It was a partnership and he needed to know how to help his woman out when he got older. Like a team, the two of us worked together and were done in no time.

"Dad, I know I'm still on punishment, but do you think I could go with Uncle Jacobi this weekend? When he brings me back home, I'll go back on punishment," Jr. asked.

"What's this weekend?" I asked, dumbfounded.

"Pre-Season starts. Uncle Jacobi got me a ticket. Remember?" *Oh yeah!* I had forgotten Jacobi had purchased their tickets months ago. Since the two of them liked the Raven's and I was more of a die-hard Skins fan, Jacobi took on the role of taking him to games. It was a good opportunity for the two of them to spend time together.

"I forgot all about that! Since you've been good and I haven't heard any complaints, I'll take you off of punishment and allow you to go." Jr gave me the biggest smile.

"I missed you, Dad!" Samir Jr said as he walked over and gave me a hug. Kid always did know how to tug at my heart.

"Miss you too, son. Now, understand that just because you are off punishment it doesn't mean you can't be put back on. You need to find a better way to act out than being disrespectful!" I wanted to cry, but I fought back the tears. I knew I couldn't be too soft in front of him.

"I understand, Dad. So, what movie are we watching?" he asked with a smirk. Since we were all having such a great night, I figured why stop at dinner. I suggested we pop some popcorn and have a family movie night, which everyone seemed excited about.

"I don't know, but since I let your mom and sister pick, we're probably in trouble!" We both laughed as we made our way into the living room with popcorn in hand.

CHAPTER 10

SKY

"Prince, come get this baby! I am not your built-in babysitter!" Before he could say anything, I hung up.

This was the third time this week that he had asked me to babysit. If it weren't for him working, I probably wouldn't have done it. I knew the boy needed his money. Otherwise, he would be begging for something, be it a babysitter or money for rent. The problem is that he got off at two o'clock and it was now four. It didn't take that long to get here from work.

"Ma, don't you think you're being a little hard on him? He's trying and you won't give him a break!" Profit was so naive, always running to his brother's rescue. Even when he was wrong. Way I saw it, Prince had made his bed and it well past time he lie in it. I wasn't going to cut him any slack just because he was my son.

Tough love.

"And that's why you have to be very careful what you say to me. He was all big and bad not too long ago—didn't need me, wasn't ever gonna need me. Now look at him." Kids always thought that they could speak to their parents any way they wanted. Until they needed you. Then, all of a sudden, their whole tune would change.

"Ma, do you ever let anything go? Forgive and move on—ain't that what you always taught us?" Profit asked as he picked up the baby and walked up the stairs. He was a good uncle, but I was secretly hoping he didn't get any ideas anytime soon.

I knew there was no need wasting my time trying to explain my view points. They would both understand in due time. And when that day comes, we'll see how they feel. Most of the time I can forgive and forget, but not when it comes to my kids. I'm never going to forget how Prince stood up for that chicken bone eating dusty hoodrat, Kim. One thing I will give her is the fact that she didn't lie. She said she wasn't doing shit when it came to that baby and she'd been true to her word. Sorry excuse for a grandmother, if you ask me. And she had the audacity to talk big shit about me, herself and her daughter.

Everyone was mad because I didn't show up to the gender reveal or baby shower. Hell, I didn't even go to the hospital when Lawanda was in labor. But, just like her, I'm true to my word. I wasn't doing anything, or being involved in anything, until that DNA test came back. Prince was hurt that I wasn't there, but he knew my reasoning. He should have been glad that his dad showed up, as reluctant as he was. Two months later the DNA test came back that Prince was the father. That's when I stepped in and started playing my role.

In fact, that same day I went to see Lil Prince. The moment I laid eyes on him, I knew he was one of ours. As expected, Kim and Lawanda weren't happy to see me. They were rolling their eyes and sucking their teeth the entire time I was holding him. Prince, protective as he is, was posted up just in case things got out of hand. I was so deeply in love with my first grandson that I was able to ignore all the shade Kim and her daughter were throwing at me.

After a couple of hours of cuddling with my pumpkin I carefully placed him in the nearby bassinet and prepared to leave. However, before doing so, I looked around to see what they had. It looked like a bunch of nothing, aside from the gifts Savonna, Serenity, and Cassey had purchased. I wasn't sure what kind of baby shower they'd had, but my guess is that it was ghetto and classless. It was probably one of those showers that everyone shows up to, empty-handed. Before exiting, I made a mental checklist of everything they needed, starting with some decent bottles, bibs, and clothes. Lawanda wasn't breast feeding, so she was using dollar store bottles, a cheap bib, and had that baby dressed a thin t-shirt.

It's time for me to escape to every baby store possible, I thought to myself as left their apartment.

For the next four hours were spent visiting every baby store I could find. My first stop was to Wal-Mart. I bought my pumpkin a three in one premium stroller, a Graco swing, a number of onesies, wash rags, towels, receiving blankets, a baby carrier, three cases of Pampers, a newborn lounger, diaper caddy, bibs, bottle warmer, bottle sterilizer, simply natural bottles, five cases of Enfamil and four cases of wipes. When I had finished, I went to *Carter's* and *Children's Place* to stock up on clothing and infant shoes.

Later that evening, I pulled up with a car load of baby stuff for my Pumpkin. I called Prince, who appeared appreciative, and told him to come outside and help me carry the stuff in. We did at least five trips before it was all stacked in their tiny apartment. But you can bet there was a completely different reaction from Lawanda and Kim. Their mouths hung wide open in disgust. I let them know without saying one word that grandma ain't no slouch! I had done more for Pumpkin in one day than they had done in two months! And one of them was the mother of that gorgeous baby.

But I didn't stop there.

When we had finished unloading everything, I had Prince take a ride with me to the furniture store. I had Prince pick out what he liked and I ordered them a bedroom set and kitchen set. Then, we went back to Wal-Mart to get some dishes, pots and pans, a microwave, utensils, a toaster, some sheets and a comforter set.

I was taken aback the moment I stepped inside their apartment. They didn't even have the basics. When they moved in, they had nothing but their clothes and a blow-up mattress. I would have figured they had gotten some things, but it didn't appear that way. I may not be Lawanda's greatest fan, but I do care how my son and grandson live.

Prince was so excited he couldn't wait to get home and tell Lawanda. I was just grateful Kim wasn't there when we got back. It must have been past time for her to go home or to the nearest club. I didn't really care where she went as long as I wasn't subject to her existence.

As I expected, Lawanda wasn't nearly as excited or grateful as Prince. The moment she found out it became, 'I was gonna get that,' 'I was gonna do that,' 'I wanted to pick out my own furniture.' Such an ungrateful hoodrat! I don't know where she thought she getting the money from. Just knowing that I'd made Prince's day was more than enough for me. She couldn't have been too bothered by the choices because every time I go over there it's the same furniture I'd purchased.

*****

"Ma, you ain't cook?" Prince asked as he walked into the kitchen looking for something to eat.

"Who am I cooking for? Most of the time, I'm here by myself. I'm tired of throwing food away." Profit worked and went to school. And when he did have free time, it was spent with his girlfriend. He was hardly ever here. Now, with John gone, the only person I had to worry about feeding was myself.

"All you have to do is call me and I'll come over and get some food. Lawanda can't cook. Maybe you could give her some lessons?" Prince suggested as he walked over to give me a hug and a kiss.

"That girl barely speaks to me and you think she wants me in her kitchen? Pshh—" I threw my hands up in the air. "The baby is upstairs with your brother. Why are you so late anyway?"

"I worked late so that I could get some extra cash to pay these bills."

Prince had been working his behind off trying to take care of the baby and Lawanda. Since she normally had the baby all day, so he would bring him over to me when he wanted to give her a break. If you ask me, she needed to get off her ass and get a damn job. They needed two incomes if they wanted to stay afloat. I tried not to meddle in their personal business because I knew I could be harsh. It was hard for me to hide the fact that I didn't like her or how she treated my son and grandson. Any time her and Prince would go at it, she would take the baby and up and move out, not allowing any of us to see him.

"How much do you need?" I asked, despite having just paid his car insurance. We knew he needed a reliable vehicle to get to and from work, so John gave him his old car and got a new one. Prince assured John that he could afford the car insurance, but he'd only made one payment. I knew John would be pissed if he found out that I'd been the one making the payments, but I didn't care.

"I got this," Prince insisted. "My check should be pretty decent this week, Ma. But thanks for looking out. I'm gonna get the baby and mess with Profit for a minute." Without another word, he ran up the stairs in the direction of his brother's bedroom.

It warmed my heart to see my son becoming a man, handling his business the best way he knew how. I was so proud of him because I never thought I would see this day. I sometimes questioned the way I raised my boys. Everyone always said that they were Mama's boys and would be stuck up my ass forever. But today—today was one of those days I wanted to pat myself on the back.

Sauntering over to the window, I peered out at the garage. I missed John and I wished he were here for him to witness this. I just may have gone too far this time. Despite our disagreements, he had never left me. I just couldn't bring myself to give into his demands. I knew my family way before him! And who in their right mind would give someone that kind of ultimatum.

I knew it was primarily my ego and pride hindering me, but I wouldn't allow myself to bow down to a man. Growing up, my mother had always told us, no matter who we marry, don't lose our voice. I refuse to be submissive—voiceless—like my sisters. I've always had a strong personality and I stand for what I believe in. If any of my siblings need me, I'm going to be there. Regardless of what my husband says.

I'm team McMillan all day, every day! That's just the way it is.

I was angry that he even thought I would choose him over my family. Angry that he gave me an ultimatum. *What type of man did I marry? I stood by him through all his infidelities! I played my role and stood in my place. So, if he's waiting for me to beg him to come home, he's got another thing coming.*

Since he left, our communication had diminished and was now a bare minimum. In the beginning, we were talking here and there. That was until we got into another heated argument. John once again started telling me that as my husband, he should always come first. I hated how he treated me as though I were stupid. He acted as though I didn't know he should come first. Of course, I knew that. What he refused to understand was that my family needed me and when my family called, especially after what we had just been through, I would drop everything to be there for them. No matter what. One thing was for certain and two things were for sure—if he divorced me, whether it be today or tomorrow, my last name would go back to McMillan because they would always be my blood family and John wouldn't.

My words must have pissed him off because now I only get text messages from him. Usually about the bills or the money that he transfers to our joint account. The few times I have tried to call, he refused to answer. Regardless, he needed to figure out what he wanted to do before I went and filed the papers myself. Which was something I said I never wanted to do. Whether he knew it or not, John was on the clock. And time was ticking. He had thirty days to come to some kind of resolution and get his ass back in this house. If not, he would find me at the courthouse, resolving it for him.

CHAPTER 11

SAVONNA

FAMILIAR SURROUNDINGS

It felt good to finally be back in my own place. Don't get me wrong, leaving Tootie's was bittersweet, but we both knew that it was time. Not only had I lost Preston, I'd lost the one human being that was closest to him.

I'll admit, I miss her company and the moments we shared. Especially since I hadn't heard from her. Not one call or text to say hello since the day I left. Of course, I couldn't put all the blame on her because I didn't try to reach out to her either. Perhaps one day in the future we'll run into one another and shoot the breeze. For now, the chapter of me and Tootie is closed.

My living situation with Tootie went left when she started entertaining Chad. There was already tension there, but that took the cake.

Chad was an unbearable pain in the ass who kept stopping by to see me. I suppose I have Angel to thank for his reappearance, a man she couldn't even stand. For the life of me, I couldn't figure out what would possess her to pick up the phone and call him. I didn't want to be bothered by anyone and thought I'd made myself clear in that regard. Unfortunately for me, Chad wouldn't take no for an answer.

Tootie would sit and talk with him for hours on end, while I'd locked myself away in my room. The two of them would laugh like they were the best of friends. I suppose it was therapeutic for her. Perhaps Chad reminded her of Preston. I don't know how, since they were nothing alike. But to each their own.

One day, Tootie suggested that Chad and I get back together. She raved about how much she loved him for me and made mention that I needed to lower my standards. I found so much wrong with her statement. For her to sit there and tell me, a broken-hearted woman, to jump on the next best thing…it violated me in more ways than I can even begin to explain. It was disrespectful. First off, I wasn't over her son. Second, a relationship was the furthest thing from my mind. And third, why would I—or should I—have to lower my standards?

That's the problem with the world now, everyone lowered their standards and agreed that it was acceptable to get treated half assed. Don't get me wrong, it's not that Chad is a bad catch. He's a wonderful gentleman. He's just not for me. What no one seems to understand is that when I say I don't want to be anybody's second wife, that's exactly what I mean. Besides, I haven't totally forgiven him for leaving me hanging. For him to cut me off the way he did was unacceptable. Friends aren't supposed to do that to one another.

Correction, I was his friend. He was my friend with intentions.

Truth be told, Chad should have never even been thinking that he had a chance with me. I never once led him on. That was his mind going to work. From the get-go I made it known that he and I were done. There was no future for the two of us. He should have known I wouldn't be interested after the man I was set to marry died.

When I finally did come around, I asked him why I should trust him. I explained that in the back of my mind I would just be wondering when he was going to run off again. He, of course, promised that he wouldn't. One thing I had come to realize since Preston's passing is that a man can't promise me shit. Every man I've ever known, expect my father, had let me down. The only positive of Chad was that when he ran off again, I would be prepared. You can't be disappointed, when you're expecting it.

He's around more now than he's ever been. Which isn't a problem for me because I need his company, but I feel no type of way. On the other hand, this might not be so healthy for him. It was cool when he had a girlfriend. Then they suddenly broke up. Of course, I would have broken up with him too. He was spending more of his time with me, than he was with her.

"Are you sure she doesn't mind you being over here?" I asked him repeatedly.

"She's fine and very understanding of the situation." Ain't no way a woman was okay with her man constantly being with another woman. It was one thing when he came to the funeral to show his respects. I could see her being okay with that. But I knew damn well she wasn't okay with him coming to see me every day.

In a way, I think I had become a project of sorts. He wanted to fix me because I was broken, but he also wanted the victory when all was said and done. I just wanted his friendship, but he consistently treated me as if I was one of his clients. The last thing I needed was a therapy session every single time I saw him.

Many people don't understand, but as difficult as it is, I've come to grips with never finding love. And given the events of late, I don't want it. I don't want anybody to love me because it just ends in heartbreak or disaster. Truthfully, I don't ever want to be in another relationship. I'm never getting married and I'm never having any children. My mothering will come from spending time with my nieces and nephews.

It was a tough lesson, but I learned it. Love costs too much and I couldn't afford it!

It seems that every time I find love, I lose myself in the process. The only way for me to keep myself together and protect my heart was to stay single. As disappointing as it was, the vision I'd always had for myself was clearly not in God's plan. And it is well within my soul. Everyone wasn't put on this Earth to be in a relationship. I've come to accept that my purpose has still yet to be discovered.

That's not to say I won't be tempted. Hell, I already feel lonely. But I'll never be lonely enough to forget everything that I've been through.

Apartment hunting was easy because I took the first decent one that I found, a small luxury apartment on 16th Street, not far from work. Assuming I ever decided to go back. I took a virtual tour online and it seemed to have everything I'd ever need: a fitness center, pool, and security. I filled out the application and was approved within thirty minutes. The place was vacant, so I moved in that same week with the help of Angel, Danielle, and Chad. Of course, they were more excited than me.

I'll admit, it was a blessing having their help. They had me damn near unpacked that same day. I only had a few boxes left and they were nothing more than miscellaneous stuff. It was a fun day and my spirits were temporarily lifted. I even laughed, which was something I rarely did lately. When they left and went home, I cried myself to sleep. Mainly because I felt so lonely, just me and a bunch of walls. Since then, however, coming home to my cozy little apartment had become my safe haven.

As disapproving as I had been in the beginning, Chad had become my rock. He and Angel have been patient with me. The complete opposite of my own family. They didn't even seem to be sympathetic. At first, they were. Now, it seems like the only thing they want me to do is get over it and get on with my life.

Well, that's not entirely true. Samir kind of understands.

My parents keep assuring me that I'm in their prayers and that I'm going to be all right. Sky and Serenity are just plain over me.

Sky is always trying to push me to do things that I don't want to do. Her answer for everything is to stay busy and keep my mind focused on anything except Preston and my grief. She can't seem to understand that I would rather deal with it now than have it come creeping up later. As for Serenity, she keeps comparing our situations, as if they are equal. Her getting shot and losing her man to a jail sentence he deserved, and me losing Preston were two very different things.

The only problem that I'm having with Chad and Angel is that they keep trying to get me to go out. I have no desire to go hang out or be around a bunch of people. I go out once a week, and that's to check on my parents. Some weeks, that's a struggle. I sit there for a couple of hours and then I go back home, back to my safe zone.

*****

BUZZ! the obnoxious sound of the buzzer alerted me to the fact that someone was here.

"Who is it?" I asked over the intercom.

"The Boogie Man!" Chad responded. I rolled my eyes as I unlocked the door, buzzed him in, and climbed back on the couch.

"Hey you," he greeted cheerily as he made his way into the kitchen with a bag of Chinese food in hand. "Savonna, you have to start eating. And before you say anything, I know you haven't eaten today." This had become the norm. Either he was in my kitchen, cooking, or bringing me something to eat. He just couldn't understand that I still had no appetite.

"I didn't realize it was so late in the day," I admitted as I glanced at the clock. Time often got away from me when I was lost in my thoughts. So, the fact that I had forgotten to eat or even get dressed for the day was nothing new.

"How long have you been sitting on that couch with the TV watching you?" he questioned, studying me closely.

What does it matter? See, this is exactly what I meant when I said he thought he was my therapist.

"Since I got up!" I snapped. *Oh, man, that food does smell good,* I thought just as my stomach growled.

"Oh yeah? Well, what did you watch?" Chad asked as he started making our plates.

"Ummmm…good question." I remember watching some of the news, but that was about it. Since then, the TV has been watching me.

"That's what I thought. You seem to do that a lot. You think too much, Vonna. Come on, come over here and eat with me!" Chad instructed, pulling out a chair for me.

I walked over and sat down at the table beside him as Chad began unpacking the food. He'd brought my favorite: sushi and shrimp lo mein. *Who's eating all of this?* I thought in disbelief. I knew I could stand to put some of my weight back on, but this was too much. Especially when I haven't been eating much as of late.

I'd barely made a dent in my plate before calling it quits, my stomach beyond full. Chad didn't say anything as we ate, which told me he had something on his mind.

"This was very good. Thank you," I said, taking a sip of my water. "Chad, I want you to know that I appreciate you and everything you've done for me. I promise, I won't ever take you for granted." Too many times people didn't take the time to tell their loved ones just how much they meant to them, an act that I had been guilty of this in the past. I found that recently, I'd been saying it far more. Perhaps too much. I know they know how I feel, but sometimes it's nice to hear it.

"You are more than welcome, Vonna. I truly believe that if the tables were turned it would be reciprocated. Though I do wish you would eat more," Chad admitted, locking eyes with me.

"You know how I do," I shrugged. "My appetite will eventually come back—" *At least I hope it will,* I thought, trying to convince myself. At the moment, I didn't care if I ate or not. Which was my first clue that I still wasn't up to par. Food had always been something I loved, so me not eating was abnormal.

"When do you think you'll be ready to go back to work?" he asked hesitantly. For some reason I felt like I was being rushed back to work by everyone around me. What no one seemed to understand was that I would be no good to any client if I couldn't even defend myself. The Prosecutor's would tear me up in the courtroom. And I wouldn't allow that.

"Do you honestly think I'm ready?" I asked, eyeing him knowingly.

"It's not up to me, Vonna. But you'll never know until you give it a try. All I'm saying is think about it. Maybe go into the office a couple times a week—at least until you're fully ready to get back into the swing of things," Chad suggested as he began packing up the remaining food.

"That's not a bad idea. I'll call Tim in the morning. Who knows, maybe they'll have a case that would allow me to do some research. "Given the way my bank account is dwindling, I should have been back to work long time ago. It certainly couldn't hurt to have a few big cases."

CHAPTER 12

SERENITY

I couldn't stop thinking about Miles and what a good time we'd had together. I didn't want him to leave. He was only supposed to be here from Friday to Monday, but he ended up staying until the following Sunday. We had over a week full of festivities that neither one of us had planned on.

He's a corny dude, not someone that I would normally hang around. Yet, I had so much more fun with him than I'd ever expected. And just when I thought things couldn't get any better, he footed the bill. Lord knew I couldn't afford half the stuff we had done. Before he left, I told him he was my best friend.

When he got into town on Friday, he spent some time with Tootie before making his way over to my house. I figured that his visit with her would be relieving, but he claimed it was everything but. According to him, it was more painful for the both of them.

They were both so used to seeing the other with Preston and that would never happen again.

Instead of the two of them doing something fun, like going out to eat or visiting the museum like I'd suggested when he said he was going to see her, they went to Preston's grave. Miles said they stood there for at least thirty minutes in complete silence.

"What was the silence like?" I asked.

"It was very heavy and filled with emotion, but I didn't cry. I couldn't cry. There was still too much anger residing inside of me that I refused to break down. It sounds strange, but going to the graveyard gave me all the closure that I needed." I nodded my head in understanding. He figured Preston had chosen what he wanted to do with his life, and by acting on it, he was finally in his eternal peace. Miles was suddenly relieved of any responsibility or guilt when it came to Preston's suicide because he realized there was nothing he could have done to stop it.

He had been struggling for so long that I was happy to know the weight had finally been lifted. As for Tootie, I could imagine it was different, being that she was his mother. According to Miles, she visits the gravesite once a week, faithfully. Which tells me that she hadn't made peace with his death. Part of her was probably feeling as though she'd failed her son. I only pray that one day she can come to terms with his death and realize that it's not her fault. I truly believe she would make a good advocate for other parents who have experienced the loss of a child by suicide. She could turn her testimony into a blessing for others.

Savonna had just picked up the older kids for the weekend when Miles got to the house and Sky had taken the baby earlier in the day. He picked me up and the two of us made our way over to Samir's. To our surprise, Samir and Cassey were also kid free. It bothered me a little to know that the kids were at my parents' house because they would never come to get mine. To me that showed favoritism, but I was determined to enjoy myself so I pushed my displeasure aside.

Samir called Jacobi and Tamela to invite them over and we all decided to have a cookout. While the men handled the grill, us ladies put together the sides. It was nothing fancy, just a simple tossed salad, baked beans, deviled eggs, and seafood salad.

While grilling, Samir and Jacobi took up djing, taking us way back with some old school music. I have to admit, they did a pretty good job. Us ladies were jamming, music on blast, while trying to remember some of our old school dances. Outside, the men were watching us through the balcony doors, laughing their asses off. One thing was for sure, we got our exercise that night. This old body of mine hadn't been worked out like that in a minute.

After we had finished eating, the rest of the evening turned into game night. We played *UNO, Trouble, Sorry, Family Feud* and *Wheel of Fortune.* We rounded out the evening with a family friendly game of shot roulette, which proved to be a very bad idea. Every single one of us was drunk on shots of Hennessey and Grey Goose.

We must have thought we were in our teens. Oh, how quickly we were reminded that we were too old for this. The hangovers hit differently than they did ten years ago.

When I awoke the next day, I was lying fully clothed on Samir's couch with a banging headache and sore as hell body. Glancing around the room, I was surprised to find Miles slumped over the recliner, Jacobi was passed out on the floor in the dining room, and Tamela was in the bathroom throwing up her guts. I'll admit, I was sick as a dog. But I didn't vomit. At that moment, all I wanted was my bed and a good 24-36 hours to sober up.

My head was pounding and I had one of them call on Jesus hangovers. You know the ones—where you just sit there and make promises to the Lord that you will never do something so stupid again if he just takes the pain and nausea away. I remember thinking over and over, *Jesus, take this away. I promise, I'll never do it again!*

Samir, who appeared to be the most sober of us all, got up and made us all breakfast. The moment the scent hit my nose my stomach roiled in protest. And just like that, my entire Saturday had been ruined.

Miles finally sobered up enough to drive me home around two that afternoon. Unfortunately, I slept on and off all day and wasn't much company until later that evening. Thankfully, Miles didn't seem to mind. He spent the day in the living room, chilling and watching movies. He seemed to be in his element. I figured he would go back over to hang out with Samir but instead, he stayed with me.

When I finally came around later that evening, the two of us took it easy, just talking. I felt bad because I knew there were a couple of spots he wanted to check out, but he insisted that he was good. Either way, we really enjoyed one another's company, strictly platonic. Though I'll admit there were a couple of intense moments that could have led to me committing adultery.

*****

Sunday came quickly and I was dreading the kids coming back home. As it turned out, it actually went pretty well. I got up that morning and Miles took me to breakfast at I-Hop. When we had finished, we went to the grocery store so that I could grab a few things for dinner. Despite my protests, Miles insisted he pay for the food. I told him that I was going to use my food stamps, but he told me to hold onto them. I couldn't believe my ears. Most people would rather take advantage and use food stamps than their actual cash money.

That was the moment I realized Miles wasn't educated on the lower income. The man had been born into money, his mother being a doctor and his father running his own business.

Miles had mentioned his love of soul food but that his mom rarely made it, so I decided to make a big country meal. Through conversation, I had learned that ham, baked mac and cheese, greens and cornbread were his favorite. I simply added in some stuffed peppers, dirty rice, oxtails and cabbage. He was so grateful and appreciative of my hard work.

Unlike many of the men I had come across, he didn't look at it as something that a woman was supposed to be doing. He simply appreciated that it was done. He was the kind of man that made it easy to want to cook for him.

The funny thing is I've never been known for being the cook in the family, but I could burn in the kitchen too. Rather than getting involved in the competition, I always left it up to the other three. They never asked me to make anything and I never volunteered, which I was perfectly fine with. I just stuck to bringing sodas. Sadly, I had a feeling that was all about to change.

I'd called everyone and invited them over to have dinner. Savonna and Sky were dropping off the kids anyway, so I figured why not have them come and eat. And since Samir, Cassey, Jacobi and Tamela were already invited, I couldn't very well leave Mom and Dad out. For the very first time, I had my entire family over for dinner.

My house was packed and so full of joy. I was elated.

As expected, everyone clowned on me, talking about how I had been holding out on them all these years, hiding my mad cooking skills. Samir even admitted to having Chinese food in the car as a backup plan. Savonna said she had eaten a little something before she left the house—just enough to hold her over until she got back home. Sky had picked up a sub on her way over, Jacobi and Tamela had an exit excuse made up with Popeyes on standby, and Mom and Dad said they came straight from church, praying the whole way. We were all laughing so hard that we had tears streaming down our faces.

"That's what y'all get for underestimating me," I chuckled.

That was a Sunday that will go down in history for me. They'd made my day. I had to take a step back so that I could take it all in. I couldn't believe my entire family had showed, no excuses. After dinner, the kids went to the bedrooms to play, no arguing or fussing. While the gentlemen were watching football, us ladies were in the kitchen switching topics like we women tend to do. And for the first time since Preston's death, Savonna seemed like her old self. At around 8 o'clock they all went home. And would you believe they didn't leave me and the kids any leftovers. They ate every morsel.

While I finished cleaning up the kitchen, Miles and the boys played until I told them it was time to get ready for bed. School awaited them in the morning. Lil Sky had been cranky all night, so I put her butt in the crib after feeding her. Serene, protective as she is, stood in the kitchen giving me the third degree about who the strange man was in our house. I assured her that Miles was a good man and that we were just friends. As expected, she had warmed up to Miles a bit by the end of the week.

The next morning came, bringing with it disappointment. I wasn't ready for Miles to leave and apparently neither was he. After I dropped the kids off at school, Miles asked me how I would feel if he stayed an extra week. Of course, I was ecstatic. And good thing too because he had already changed his flight to the following Monday.

That entire week proved to be an adventurous one. We took the kids bowling, skating, to the movies, Dave and Busters, the National Zoo, and the Museum of African American History. It felt like a much-needed vacation without actually leaving. Miles had done more for my children in a week than any man ever had.

One night, while we were talking, I told him that when I grew up, I wanted to be just like him. He had spent so much money on us, it was ridiculous. But it wasn't the money that meant the most. It was his time.

Miles was a breath of fresh air and I hated to see him leave because it was back to this boring everyday life that I live. *I wish Iron was home,* I thought.

I had been catching hell from him because I had been too caught up with Miles and the kids to even be bothered with him. I probably only spoke to him twice the whole time Miles was here. He had been blowing my phone up, but I just kept ignoring the calls. We were all having so much fun and I didn't want it ruined by his negativity. Every time he called Miles would tell me to answer it. I simply shrugged it off and assured him that I would talk to him later.

However, now that Miles was gone, Iron was giving me the blues. I opted not to say anything about his visit because I knew he would have a fit if he discovered how close the two of us were. And if he ever found out that he had stayed here at the house—I would be all kinds of bitches and whores. Some things were just better left unsaid. Especially when it came to Iron.

CHAPTER 13

SAMIR

"Man, all this family shit has got her going crazy!" I'd been listening to Jacobi go off for the last forty-five minutes. He drove over here all frantic, interrupting my peace and quiet. Something I hadn't had in quite a while. Cassey had taken the kids out, so I could have the house to myself for a while and here comes his paranoid ass.

Apparently, Tamela had baby fever and he was going crazy at the thought of becoming a father. I don't know why he was so worried. He was more than fit to be a father and kids loved him.

"Are you saying you don't want kids? Or you're just worried about the timing?" I had to ask because nothing he was saying made any sense. They were married and both of them were stable enough to support a child, so I didn't understand what the problem was.

"Man, I don't know. I'm still not used to being a husband! And now she wants me to be a daddy! I never even wanted a wife. She just ain't getting none," he said.

As if that's ever gonna happen.

Jacobi was acting like this was a catastrophe. I could see if Tamela was just some random chick trying to have a baby out of wedlock. But she wasn't. That was his wife. And withholding sex from his wife would only create a wedge in their marriage.

"Man, sit yo ass down and take a deep breath! It's about time for you to have a few of your own. You'll be just fine! Trust me. Besides, I want to be able to spoil my nephew or niece like you had done with these two that I have."

Jacobi had been giving my two whatever the hell they wanted from the moment they were born. Even when I tell him not to. He'd opened savings accounts for both of them with their names on them the day they were born. He'd even promised Jr. a car when he was old enough to drive. Needless to say, I've been waiting for my opportunity to return the favor. Little did he know, I was gonna piss him off badly.

"A few? Oh, hell no! You know what it is? It's this damn family always asking when we're gonna have some kids. Thanks to y'all, I'm fucked! I knew I should have never bought her around. I should have known it would only be a matter of time before her and Cassey were all buddy, buddy." I knew Cassey was going to get the charge. However, in this case, it was true. Cassey and Tamela had been hanging out a lot lately. Which I was loving. It kept me from having to hang with her all the time and let me do me a bit more.

"I said calm down before you have a stroke. You'll be no good to the kids in that condition, *Daddy*!" I said, bursting into laughter. I had to admit that I got a kick out of agitating Jacobi. He acted like he had all the worst problems in the world. He doesn't realize just how good he has it. You ask me, his life is pretty damn good. If only he knew—he better count his blessings before them real sorrows hit.

"Samir, this is not a joke! I'm coming to you, man to man. I'm not ready!" Jacobi finally sat down, all the stressful wrinkles in his forehead working overtime.

"Well, you better get ready. Remember, man, happy wife, happy life. Just give the woman what she wants."

Jacobi needed to work on his communication skills with his wife if he intended to make things work. If I had to guess, he hadn't even discussed his concerns with her. I knew my boy well enough to know that he was coming to me in an effort to avoid talking to her. You ask me, they should have been clear on what they both wanted and expected in the future before getting married.

"That's not fair! They need to change that phrase. If husband ain't happy, then he's going to be a was-band!" I damn near fell out of my chair from laughing so hard. This dude was so damn funny. He would have been a good stand-up comedian. What made it even more hilarious was the fact that he was dead serious.

"Man, you are so damn stupid. Marriage is both give and take. It's a lot of compromising. I promise you, having a baby by your wife is not the end of the world. You want to go on a road trip?" I asked in an attempt to change the subject and distract him for a bit because this was a subject Jacobi and I would never see eye-to-eye on.

As of late, my mind has been thinking about taking a guy's trip. When Miles was here, I told him not to be surprised if he found me out in his neck of the woods.

"I'm down! Where and when?" Jacobi sat up straight, anxiously waiting on my answer. If I didn't know any better, I'd say he was down to go today.

"Charlotte—to see Miles. I figured we could drive down and spend a few days. I'm thinking about leaving in two weeks–on a Friday. I'd be coming back on Monday." An impromptu road trip was something I hadn't done in a very long time. Usually, Cassey, the kids and I traveled together as a family. I just hoped she didn't give me any smack when I mentioned my plans to her. I figured after the year that I was having, I deserved to have some fun in my life.

"Bet, I'm with it! I'll let Tamela know," he said excitedly as he got up to leave, his entire mood having shifted since mentioning our getaway. "Since we're on the subject, is it just me or did Miles and Serenity seem like they were a couple?" Jacobi asked as he reached the door.

"I think he likes her, but he's not really her type. He's not thugged out enough. She ain't gonna do nothing but put him in the friendzone." I love my sister, but she needed to grow up and get a real man. A man like Miles would be a pleasant addition to the family. Especially coming from her. And I know we would all welcome him with open arms.

"She needs to get it together and let them knuckleheads stay in the streets! She ain't learned nothing yet." Jacobi shook his head and walked out without so much as a goodbye.

Damn, he could have said bye or at least see ya later. Rude ass!

As soon as I got comfortable on the couch, John called. Apparently, Sky's crazy ass had sent him divorce papers. I ended up being on the phone with him for over an hour. He was going on and on about his issues with Sky. For the most part, I'd been sitting back and minding my own business, hoping things between them would work out on their own.

Obviously, that wasn't going to happen.

My sister certainly had a lot of nerve. I don't know who in the hell she thought was going to put up with her, if not John. The two of them needed to work through their issues and get back together. They were two stubborn human beings that loved each other, but both refused to bend. Love was a give and take...someone had to give a little in order to make things work.

If I had to play devil's advocate, I'd lean towards Sky being the one that needs to bed. That man was her husband and he should come first. Granted, I probably feel that way because I'm a man and can feel his pain. If Cassey had done me the way Sky did John, Sky would be talking shit from here to L.A. *Maybe I need to give her a different perspective so that she can understand where he's coming from?* I wondered.

On the flipside, I understood Sky feeling the need to be there for us. If any of my sisters were to call on me, no matter the hour, I would be there in an instant. Your family is your rock and that's something I would expect John to understand. John knew how Sky was before he married her. I don't know why would expect that to change. Sometimes you just have to know what battles to pick. And I'm not entirely sure this is one of them.

After listening to him, it occurred to me that all he wanted was to feel acknowledged, no matter what was going on in her life. He felt ignored, like he didn't matter. I'll admit, my sister can be selfish. What's crazy is that it's usually only with him. I've told Sky on several occasions to never make a man feel like he's not needed. And she'd done exactly that.

She had belittled John for years. The man couldn't even be a part in raising his own sons. I told him years ago that he was a better man than me. I would have left her long ago. Ain't no way I was living with someone that was supposed to be my partner, paying all the bills, but couldn't have a say in how my kids were raised. I mean, where the hell were his balls? Sky walked all over him from day one because he allowed it. And that was on him.

John understood that Sky sent those divorce papers as a ploy to get him to come home. Unfortunately for her, the plan backfired because he actually planned on signing them. He was calling her bluff. Both of them are playing Russian roulette with their marriage. Neither of them wanted a divorce, they were just trying to see who would break first. They were both playing Russian roulette with their marriage when what they really needed was an intervention from their own stupidity.

For a while, they had been doing well and you could actually feel the love between them. They had been getting along and enjoying one another. Which was precisely what they needed to get back to. The more they allowed this to linger on, the worse it would get. In their case, absence was certainly not making the heart grow fonder. In fact, it was making the both of them more bitter. Shit was ridiculous! We were all far too old for this kind of nonsense.

I'm going to try and talk to Sky, but it isn't going to be today. I've had more than enough marriage counseling sessions for one day. I have no idea how my parents did this, it's exhausting.

CHAPTER 14

SKY

"Sky don't you think that you're taking this a bit too far?" Baby sis had no idea how hard it was being married to that asshole. I wasn't the one who took it too far, he left me! I'm just so over his whining. It's worse than a woman. What pissed him off was the fact that he wanted things his way and his way only. When I didn't give in, he snapped. Well, I hate to break it to him, but he can't get all my attention all the time. Hell, we have a grandbaby that requires less attention than him. He whines worse than a woman.

"I agree with Savonna, Sky. Go talk to your husband and work this shit out!" Neither Serenity nor Savonna were hearing me. My husband didn't want to talk to me. I'd been trying since he left. *How many times do I have to tell them this? My whole family is going crazy! Nobody is listening!*

"I CAN'T TALK TO SOMEONE THAT DOESN'T WANT TO TALK TO ME!" I shouted, hoping to finally get my point across. Everybody is saying 'Sky, Sky, Sky.' Well, what about 'John, John, John?' None of them are in his ear telling him what he should be doing. And why is that? Because everything is *my* fault. Never mind the fact that *HE* left *ME*. Just because I was the one that sent the divorce papers, doesn't mean I was the one to blame. They just couldn't seem to understand that.

"Let me ask you a question—have you told your husband that you love him and want him to come home?" Savonna asked. "Have you told your husband that you miss him? Have you asked him out on a dinner date? How exactly are these conversations going?" *Here we go again with Savonna and her love begging ass.*

Savonna was one of those that was into pacifying a grown man. That wasn't me. I wasn't going to beg. Either you're with me or you're not!

"He knows that I love him. I shouldn't have to tell him. And he also knows that the door is open for him to come home," I snapped as I pulled the biscuits from the oven.

My sisters had begged me to make some chicken and dumplings. Which, of course, I couldn't say no to. I was just waiting on the biscuits so that we could eat. With John out of the house, I had no one left to cook for. It was just me. As such, I was only cooking by request. Don't get me wrong, I wanted to cook, but it seemed like such a waste. So, you can imagine how happy I was when Savonna called and asked me to make dinner. It gave me a reason to be in the kitchen.

"That's not what Savonna asked you! Sky, you're dancing around the questions. There's nothing wrong with asking him to come home. Do you always have to be so stubborn?" Usually, I could get Serenity to be on my side. However, it appeared that wasn't going to happen tonight. As such, I decided to go into quiet mode. *These two came over here to gang up on me and I'm not trying to hear it. I'll just set up this table and we can eat in silence. I have nothing more to say about John and I. What's done is done.*

"So, Serenity, you and Miles seem to be getting along well," Savonna prodded. "What's up with that?" I sighed, grateful for the change in subject. To be fair, though, I also wanted to know.

Every time I call Serenity, she's either on the phone with him or he's beeping in. She claims they're just really good friends, but I'm not buying it. Something more was going on, I just wasn't sure what yet.

"Mmmmmm!" Serenity held her hand up for us to wait until she had finished chewing her food. "He's not my type, but we get along really well. It's crazy how I can just sit on the phone with him for hours."

"What about you, Savonna? Are you going to give Chad another chance?" I asked. Since she put Serenity on the spot, I decided to put her on the spot. She may not have realized it, but I was well aware of her little getaway to Mexico with him. I would ask how the trip was, but since I wasn't supposed to know, I decided to dig for some information. With any luck, she'd slip up. I would have been happier about it if she had let her family know her whereabouts before leaving the country.

I mean, who does that? For the moment, I would bite my tongue and wait for her or someone else to spill the beans. Eventually, it would have to come up. I didn't want to put miss little loose lips Angel on front street because then she would never tell me anything again.

"Nice try, never going to happen. I'm done with men and relationships. It doesn't even interest me." I never thought I would see the day my little sucka for love sister would just give up. I may be going through it, but relationships aren't that bad. I could only hope she changed her mind. I can tell you right now, if me and John should divorce, he will not be my last stop. I'm going back out there on the dating scene. Lord knows it's been years, but I'm open to giving it a shot if the opportunity presents itself.

"Yep, her heart and legs are closed indefinitely," Serenity half-joked. "I ain't mad at cha! Lord knows I have these kids to raise so I can't afford to go to jail!" While she said it jokingly, I knew Serenity was serious. She told me a while back that if the next man hurt Savonna she was gonna kill him. And trust when I tell you that she is crazy enough to try it.

On one hand, I understood where she was coming from because I didn't want to see her hurt again either. But on the other, I wanted to see my little sister happy again. This new Savonna—I don't much care for her. I want the old one back.

"Oh, look who's talking! We feel the same about you."

Just then, the doorbell rang. I wasn't expecting any company, so I got up to see who it was. When I opened the door, I was shocked to find Samir and Cassey standing in front of me.

"Hey, Sis," Samir and Cassey said in unison, flying right past me and straight into the kitchen. *Now, I wonder who had a big mouth and told them that I was cooking,* I thought to myself with a chuckle.

"Are y'all hungry?" I asked sarcastically as I strolled back into the kitchen to find they were already filling their plates.

"Uh, yeah, I don't know why you thought you were going to make dumplings and not invite us," Samir laughed. I had forgotten that the master chef couldn't make dumplings. It was too far out of his league.

Before I knew it, I had a full house. Which didn't bother me in the least.

Profit came in and joined us after he got off work. Then, Prince walked in and shocked everybody. I did him the courtesy of filling everyone in on his new domestic violence case that he managed to pick up after he and that hoodrat got into it. She placed a restraining order on him so he was unable to go home until this mess was resolved.

According to my son, they got into a heated argument over her having a bunch of people in the apartment every day. Because she decided to turn their place into a party house, he'd been subject to loud music and a bunch of drunk folks. And if you ask me, I'm damn near a hundred that there's been some weed smoking going on up in there too. The last couple of times I picked up the baby, he smelled like a marijuana dispensary. When I finally questioned him, he gave me the runaround and acted as if I were stupid. It's like he forgot that I'm married to a weed head and that I know what it smells like.

In the end, I let it go. They're the parents and they had to make the decisions they saw fit for their family. I'm only the grandmother, so all I can do is speak wisdom. It's up to him and that hoodrat what they do with it.

Prince has been busting his ass, working ten to twelve hours a day just to make ends meet. Which was more than I could say for her food stamp having ass. Since that's about all she can contribute. She's more than capable of working, but she refuses. And, of course, Prince sees nothing wrong with it because he never saw me work. But, like I told him, I didn't work because I didn't have to. Our situation was totally different from theirs. Lawanda's young. She should want to work. Even if it's nothing more than a part time job to help out.

When John and I were their age, I'd be damned if I would have watched him struggle. My degree would have kicked in real quick. But that hoodrat—she didn't even have an education to back her up. The little heffa should be grateful and appreciative of everything she has. The way these young men are set up today, you're lucky if they're even willing to be involved. And you can forget being a provider.

The way I see it, if a man is paying all the bills, the least you could do is cook and clean. By all means necessary, keep him happy! Prince saw how I made sure his father had a hot meal and clean home to come home to. John never had any complaints about me being a stay-at-home Mom. On Sunday, I even made sure to lay his clothes laid out for the week.

He shouldn't have had to argue with her, but when I think about where she came from, the poor girl really doesn't know any better. That woman she came from couldn't have taught her nothing. I warned Prince about that from the get-go, but he wouldn't listen to me. I suggested that we go for full custody the moment the DNA test confirmed that baby was his. My grandson shouldn't be growing up in that type of environment. Of course, Prince thinks that's taking it too far. He just doesn't realize that the way a child is raised has an impact, and if we can get to his son while he's little, there's still hope.

Savonna tried to explain the severity of the charges he was facing. Still, somewhere in his head, he feels like this will just blow over and they'll be magically playing house again. As expected, Samir dug into his ass. He told him that once a woman gets you locked up, it becomes a threat to his livelihood. And in turn, the life of his child. We're all against them getting back together, but you can't tell kids these days nothing.

Prince explained that he tried to be discreet and called her into the bedroom. He told her that he wanted everyone out so that he could get some rest for work in the morning. Pissed that he was ruining her fun, Ms. Hoodrat started belittling him in front of her friends, acting like she was the one holding down the household. He said he called her out of her name, but I know that meant he called her the bitch that she was being. Which was when she became irate and started swinging on him. In an effort to protect himself, he grabbed her by both hands and pushed her away from him. She ended up losing her footing and fell into the wall. Which was when she decided to call the police.

So, while Prince gets locked up, she gets to play victim. We all told him it wouldn't last long because she was going to need him to pay them bills and help take care of the baby. Savonna said the best he could hope for is that Lawanda doesn't show up to court and the state's attorney is forced to drop all charges. However, in the event that she carried on with the nonsense, she assured us that Prince had a good case. And I believed her.

Knowing my sister the way I did, I knew she would sock it to her ass and pull out all the stops. By the time Savonna was done, the judge would be giving Prince full custody. The hoodrat may not know it now, but she was messing with the wrong family!

CHAPTER 15

SAVONNA

Ever since my trip to Mexico, I'd felt revived. Chad and I took a quick four-day vacation, strictly platonic. The clear water, the beaming sun—it did me some good. When he initially suggested we get out of here and head to Mexico, I thought he was crazy. He kept insisting I needed some time away. But I had to admit, Chad was right again. At first, I was reluctant because I didn't want to risk stepping away from my comfort zone. However, I also didn't want to send mixed signals.

I was so relaxed, sitting on those white sandy beaches without a care in the world. For the first time in a long time, my mind and body were both at peace. It was a feeling I hadn't had in a very long time. I wish I could have stayed a good month or so, but I knew work wouldn't let me be that great.

Being back at work, despite my protests, had been keeping me busy. I was still very cautious about how I moved these days. Besides work and having playdates with my nieces and nephews, I still didn't go anywhere. The sole source of my social life came from Angel, Danielle, Chad, and my family. For the time being, keeping to myself had been my number one priority. Privately, I still have my melt downs. However, they were getting better. Publicly, I was able to put on a brave face. I liked to call it my reality stage.

I still had no interest in men or anything to do with dating. To be honest, I'd grown quite comfortable being alone and that's exactly the way I wanted it to stay. My family thought that in time I might change my mind. What they didn't know was that I would have to be willing and open to it. And at the moment, I wasn't.

I'd also found that my prayers were different these days. Before Preston, I used to pray for God to send me my soulmate. Now, I pray to God that he keeps me pure and lets no man near my heart. Given my track record, playing it safe seemed like the way to go. I wasn't sure that I could take any more chances. I just didn't feel like I had it in me.

The funny thing about this whole transition I found myself in, was that Chad was the only one who understood me. I knew somewhere down the line he would try and strike up a relationship conversation but so far, he hadn't brought it up. To be honest, I half expected it when we went to Mexico. As luck would have it, he was cool beans, no mention of relationships at all.

Since we'd been back, he'd gone out on a few dates. Of course, I gave him some pointers. I admit, I was loving the space that the two of us were in. But I was also very aware that he was capable of leaving me again. The difference is that I was prepared this time.

I'd been shown in the worst way possible how one-minute things could be so beautiful and the next, so very ugly. I no longer put a huge emphasis on having high expectations when it came to humans. I'd learned that you could never be too sure of what a person would or would not do. I also learned that the only person I could count on, besides myself, was the Lord. Looking back, I could completely understand why my mother stood on solid ground when she would say that.

*****

"Hey, daydreamer, what's out that window that has your attention?" Tim asked as he stepped into my office, startling me. I'd noticed he'd been a little extra these days. Three to four times a day he would check in on me. However, from the look on his face, it appeared I needed to be the one checking on him.

"Nothing…just in my zone." I knew I needed to be working on the new case they dropped in my lap, but I couldn't seem to focus. Apparently, there was kind of family dispute between a mother and her daughter. From what I have gathered, the daughter has money now and her mom felt like she was entitled to it.

I mean, really, who's got time for that kind of drama? It's no wonder the rain distracted me. Granted, I've always loved to watch the rain. It helped to calm my spirit.

"Do you mind if I have a seat?" Tim asked. I nodded, motioning for him to take a seat. Regardless of what was going on in my life, I would never turn this man away. He'd been there for me through thick and thin. So, the way I saw it, I owed him.

"What's the matter?" I asked as I sat up from my relaxed state to let Tim know that he had my full attention.

"I lost in court today and I'm beating myself up because I know the guy is guilty as hell!" Tim dropped his head to his chest in defeat. As attorney's, one of the worst things that can happen to us is we lose in court. It makes you feel like such a failure after putting in all that time, preparing. And this case was no different. Tim had been working on this case for quite some time and he was confident he would win, given all the evidence that he had.

"Shit!" I muttered, knowing this wouldn't be good for his mental well-being.

This was a high-profile case that the entire world was following. So many people were depending on him to get a guilty verdict. Beverly Caple had been found strangled to death a couple of years ago after being gang raped. What made the case so bizarre was that her son was allegedly part of the gang that raped her.

According to one of her attackers that had come forward, Beverly was walking through the park when a group of young men attacked her. He swore that her son had no idea that it was his mother that was being raped. He only found out when he walked up for his turn and saw that it was his mother looking up at him. He flipped out. Knowing he would never be able to face her, he strangled her.

"I don't know how or why the jury came up with a not guilty verdict. It's mind boggling. All the evidence was right there in front of them. Even Judge Hamlett seemed stunned." One could only hope that Tim didn't choke on the closing argument. If he did, it wouldn't have helped his case.

"Tim," I muttered, grabbing his hand. "Remember when I lost my first case and I cried like a baby. I just knew the nurse was guilty of killing that baby. No one could have convinced me otherwise. And do you remember what you said to me?" To this day, I hold onto the words he spoke to me many years ago. For today, I needed him to take his own advice.

"I told you to dry up your tears, that we couldn't catch every criminal. I told you that it likely wouldn't be the last case you lost and that some things are for God to handle. I assured you that she didn't get away with anything. Why? Because we walk by faith and not by sight!" When Tim told me that, I knew what he was saying. But that didn't mean I wanted to hear it. That case nagged at my soul.

Two months later, that same nurse was charged with three other negligence cases. She ended up getting life in prison. So, while she may have gotten off on my case, she couldn't escape the wrath of the God that I serve.

"Exactly! While he may have gotten away from you this time, he will get caught up in something else. I certainly wouldn't want to be him. Can you imagine waking up every single day knowing that you killed your mother? He's already in prison, mentally!" That young man will never have peace of mind. Whether Tim knew it or not, he never needed a guilty plea. That young man's mind will eat him up. He won't be able to live with himself.

"How are you, Savonna? You seem like you're coping better these days. Although you know what they say—looks can be deceiving." Even on his worst day, he was still more concerned about my well-being than what he was dealing with. *Now, that's what you call a true friend. Given the way he was feeling, Tim could have easily bypassed me. Instead, he took the time to ask me how I was feeling.*

"I'm okay. Getting a little better every day. How are the wife and kids?" I knew that if I didn't ask about his family, Tim wouldn't bring them up. He used to talk about them all the time, but since Preston's passing, he'd been very tight-lipped. I think maybe he thought he was protecting my feelings. Truth was I didn't feel any particular type of way. He had a wife and kids long before Preston came into the picture and it was my job to make him feel that level of comfort again.

"Everyone is fine. They ask about you all the time. You should stop by and have dinner with us sometime this week!" Tim appeared excited at the thought of having me over. *How could I possibly let him down?* I would have been there the moment he asked, but he'd never extended the invite. *So what if the last time I was there was with Preston? Everyone still thinks they're dealing with the broken Savonna, but I'm as fixed as I'm going to get.*

"As long as I get my favorites, I'm there. You just let me know what day." Tim knew I would only come if his wife made her famous meatballs from scratch and homemade sauce. Her food was so good. Everything she made tasted like it came from straight Italy.

"Okay," he chuckled. "I'll talk to the wife and let you know what day. Thanks for the pep talk." Tim stood from his chair and prepared to exit. "Oh, by the way, here is what landed on my desk today," he added, tossing a file onto my desk's top.

"What's this?" I asked, puzzled. I hadn't asked for another case, so I had no idea what it could have possibly been.

"Your sister's husband filed an appeal." Tim shook his head and walked out of my office.

My sister's husband? An appeal? Tim had to be mistaken. *The only sister I have that's having issues with her husband is Sky, and there ain't no reason for him to be filing an appeal because their divorce hadn't gone that far yet.*

I opened up the file and scanned the documents inside. At first glance it appeared that crazed animal that had shot my sister had filed an appeal for early release. *That smartass,* I thought. *Tim knows Serenity and that psycho aren't married.* But as I continued to read, I realized how little I knew about my own sister. There in black and white, the paperwork stated that the defendant and plaintiff were, in fact, married. Which was precisely what he was using as a part of his defense.

My dumb ass sister had smacked me in my face once again and I was beyond livid. *How could she marry him? After everything he had done to her, how could she have gone off and married that crazy ass psycho.*

CHAPTER 16

SAMIR

"When you get home, I'm going on my girls' trip! You left me here alone with these two badasses!" Cassey shouted, a little salty about the little trip I'd gone on. Ever since I had gotten home, she'd been socking it to me. I even had to do the grocery shopping for the week, which was something that she normally did. We each had our shared responsibilities but wifey had been chilling and full of excuses. It's all good, I could suck it up.

"They're only bad with you. I don't have those problems. What do you want, woman?" I asked jokingly. I was on my lunchbreak and I usually spent that hour talking to her anyway.

"Well, me and the kids want you to take us out for dinner tonight. Longhorn sounds good." I knew I couldn't say no even if I wanted to because I was still climbing out of the dog house. So, for the time being, everything was going to be a yes. Though I had to admit, I loved how she threw the kids in there, despite the fact that they were in school.

"You do know—"

"Yes, your food tastes better!" Cassey rudely interrupted me, finishing my sentence. *It's the truth. They didn't call me Chef Samir for nothing,* I thought to myself.

"Well, I'm just saying. But if that's what you want to do, I'm fine with it. Be ready by six," I confirmed before hanging up the phone. Women were something else—they always seemed to know just how to get what they wanted.

I couldn't lie, I kind of felt bad leaving Cassey here with the kids. Of course, if I were being honest, that guilt didn't actually hit me until Jacobi and I were almost home. The two of us stopped at the nearest florist shop to pick our wives up a dozen roses and some balloons. It was my idea, but Jacobi followed suit. Which worked out in his favor because his car was parked at my house when we pulled in. Tamela just happened to be hanging out with her newly acquired BFF. Hell, I saw Tamela more than I did Jacobi as of late because our wives were always doing something together.

I knew better than to come home empty handed, so I walked in bearing gifts that I'd picked up Cassey and the kids from the mall in Charlotte. Most important were the greetings that we got. The hugs and kisses we received—you would have thought we'd been deployed overseas for a couple of years instead of a few states away for a couple days. Even my kids seemed happy to see me. I always missed them, but it was nice to have them miss me for a change.

Although they were very appreciative, Cassey still knew me a little too well. Right after Tamela and Jacobi left she turned and narrowed her eyes on me. "Guilt must have been eating your ass up." I couldn't help the laugh that escaped me.

I could see why she might be angry. We always traveled together. However, given everything that had happened as of late, I needed to get the hell away. She let me go without giving me any issues, but I don't think she thought out the consequences of that decision.

"I'm sorry for being selfish and leaving you alone with the kids," I apologized.

It wasn't until that moment I realized just how much she has been through this past year, taking care of the kids and me. She had been doing all the cooking and cleaning while I was down and out. Everything fell on her, but she stuck it out. I owed it to her to be grateful. Any other woman would have probably left me, wife or not. I know it couldn't have been easy, yet she still did it.

Now that I think about it, Cassey was the one that could have used a vacation from us. Instead, I had the nerve to take my ass to Charlotte and leave her here at home to deal with everything all over again.

She didn't know it yet, but I had every intention of making it up to her. In a big way.

Jacobi and I had talked about and decided we were going to send the two of them on a surprise vacation for an entire week, an all-inclusive cruise to the Virgin Islands. Cassey wasn't going to see it coming, but I couldn't think of anyone more deserving. Even better? This little vacation would make us even. I would no longer have one up on her.

Maybe I'll give her the ticket tonight while we're at dinner, I thought. I would just have to run it by Jacobi so he had a heads up and could make sure he told Tamela. Lord knows, Cassey would call her the moment she found out.

My only hope was that they had as much fun as we did. I regret how I went about it, but that trip helped to remind me of my college days—kid free, wife free—the cuffs were finally off and I was able to let loose for a bit. And I must admit, Charlotte had some beautiful women. Those southern beauties kept me more entertained than I would have ever expected. Of course, I didn't dare touch anything. I'd learned my lesson…stepping out didn't bring nothing but more problems. Ain't nobody got time for that. I'd rather stick with my one pain in the butt.

But that didn't mean I damn sure couldn't look. And boy, did I.

When we got there, Miles had an entire itinerary laid out for us. The first night was spent at the strip club. Miles got a couple of lap dances while me and Jacobi watched. I've never really been big on strip clubs or strippers. There was nothing that turned me on about naked women dancing on a pole while waiting on the highest bidder. Don't get me wrong, I'm not knocking their hustle, it just ain't for me.

Now, my wife getting on a pole just for me during one of our freak sessions—yeah, that turned me on. Out of the three of us, I knew I was the only one that didn't enjoy it. However, I did participate in giving a few big booty women some dollars. And I was more than happy when the guys said it was time to leave.

From there, Miles took us to a bar that a friend of his owned. It was small, but jumping. Miles introduced us to damn near everyone in the bar. While the music was different from what we were used to, the vibe appeared to be more of a family atmosphere. Everybody was cool with one another and made Jacobi and I feel welcome. We were so comfortable that we let our guard down completely. Jacobi and I sat at the bar, running our mouths with the bartender, Kenya, and her man, Chris, while Miles got his dance on. I learned that Chris was actually from Maryland, but had been living in Charlotte for the last five years. We spent the next several hours drinking and talking like we'd known each other our whole lives.

That was until I had one drink too many. The up-side was that I didn't pay for a single one of them.

I don't know how long we had been there before we staggered our drunk asses out of there. I was just grateful that Miles only lived a couple of blocks away. Had it had been any further, we would have been taking an Uber or Lyft. Honestly, we probably should have done that anyway.

Miles somehow managed to get us all back to his place safe and sound, but not before that alcohol took hold. His loose lips started telling us how much he was in love with Serenity. While I'd had my suspicions that he liked her when he visited us, I didn't know it was to this extent. the two of us told him to shoot his shot. Lord knows I wouldn't mind him being a part of the family. He was genuinely a decent guy, exactly what Serenity needed.

Day two was filled with even more festivities. Miles had us up and at 'em early that morning. We started out with breakfast at the Flying Biscuit Cafe. I gotta say, those biscuits and gravy were a force to be reckoned with. That one recipe that I needed to learn, and quickly. I could certainly see why they were rated one of the best spots in Charlotte.

From there, we did a little bit of sightseeing. I couldn't help but notice how clean the city was compared to DC's dirty ass streets. Damn shame given that we lived right in the nation's capital. I suppose you can't let that fool ya. As we all know, looks can be deceiving.

Later that afternoon, Miles took us to SouthPark Mall where we got to do a little bit of shopping. I copped a couple of t-shirts for myself, but of the money I spent was on Cassey and the kids. I don't go to the mall often but when I do, I act a fool and end up overdoing it. Which was exactly what I did.

I came out looking like it was Christmas, bags full of gifts. Jacobi and Miles were ready to leave long before me, but I was still popping in and out of stores. In a way, it felt like I was spoiling my family. Which was something that I hadn't done in a very long time. I partially blame that on Cassey. All that shopping she used to do…it turned me off completely. I just thank God that we're past that.

When I had finished at the mall, the three of us went on one of Charlotte's Brew Cruises. I would have never guessed that Charlotte had so many breweries. I remember thinking, *Why in the world did Miles bring us here?*

Jacobi and I were known for putting down some beer, so a brew cruise was right up our alley. Unfortunately for him, Miles couldn't hang with beer kings and tapped out halfway through. Jacobi and I, on the other hand, we damn near tried every beer they had. It was fun. Beer usually doesn't do anything for us, we just liked the taste, but we were both feeling it pretty quickly. I assumed it was the fact that we'd had so many different flavors.

By the time we were done drinking all that beer we for sure had to coat our stomachs. We ended up a a place called Midwood Smokehouse. Best barbecue I'd ever had in my life. That barbecue would honestly make you wanna smack yo momma! It was tender, juicy and flavored so well. The beer had me so bloated that I was unable to finish all my food, which pissed me off to no end. I may have even had a few choice words for Miles that weren't so nice when I told him he had done all this backwards. Damn beer tour could have waited!

To round out a fun-filled day, we ended the evening at the game: Charlotte Hornets vs Boston Celtics. I knew he had to have paid a pretty penny for those tickets. Especially since our seats were right above the court, Section 101. Miles was clearly showing off for us, but I didn't mind in the least. I told him that if he kept this type of hospitality up, I'd be back every week.

He may not have known it, but I loved basketball like I loved to cook. I didn't particularly care for the Hornets or the Celtics but if it had anything to do with basketball, I was all in, no matter the team.

Miles was a big Hornets fan, so when they ended up losing by two, Jacobi and I couldn't help but clown the hell out of him.

Overall, it was a good game and we all had a blast. The only downfall to the entire trip was that I didn't know we would be going to a basketball game, so I couldn't go dressed, top to bottom, in Wizard's gear.

CHAPTER 17

SAVONNA

Serenity needed to stop opening up old wounds that hadn't even settled in my spirit yet. I had finally put Preston out of my mind and was trying to move forward before being thrown three steps back.

Over the last week I'd had no appetite and I couldn't sleep well, tossing and turning all night long. My horrific nightmares were back with a vengeance and rolling steady. It had gotten so bad that I'd actually been making emergency phone calls to my therapist throughout the night. I'm sure by now she's grown quite sick of me.

And if that weren't enough, my panic attacks were also back.

Each night, the same nightmare was the same. The only difference was that Serenity and the kids had been added to it. In my dream I would turn on the news and see the headline: **WOMAN**

FOUND DEAD ALONGSIDE THREE YOUNG CHILDREN AND A TODDLER.

The news anchor went on to say that all five victims had suffered gunshot wounds to the head. And that's when my entire world stopped spinning. I watched with bated breath as pictures were displayed on the television screen. Panicked, I ran outside screaming Preston's name, only to find him hanging in the garage. That's when I would wake up, my body covered in sweat.

Unable to go back to sleep for fear of having the same dream, I would force myself to stay up until I couldn't keep my eyes open. Then, like a broken film reel, the images would play in my mind again.

My therapist seemed to think that if I confronted Serenity it would help. According to her, the dreams have returned because I'm holding her secret inside and that's what's causing part of my anxiety. At this point, I was willing to try anything. Except crack. I wasn't willing to try that. Though if I didn't get some sleep soon, that may very well become an option.

Melatonin would put me to sleep for a good fifteen minutes before I was right back up. I had been doing so good on my own, so the last thing I wanted to do was get back on the meds. I had just gotten weaned off of them.

I told myself that I would not be the one to tell my parents and siblings what Serenity had been up to. I refused to be the reason we all found ourselves in the midst of another family war. Last time that happened, too many feelings had been hurt. I decided it would be best to spare everyone the heartache and keep my mouth shut. The problem was that forced me to suffer in silence. Well, mostly. I don't know what I would have done if it weren't for my therapist. She was the only one who knew the turmoil I was carrying with me.

Our parents were up there in age and I wasn't so sure my father could survive another one of Serenity's misguided decisions. Our parents may be holy, but they're also human. So, if she thinks that this is something they will run in a corner and pray about, she's sadly mistaken. Little did she know, Dad was in cahoots with Samir and Jacobi the last time. If that were to happen again—well, let's just say I could see him getting his hands dirty.

And then there was Sky. If she were to find out, Serenity could go ahead and forget she ever had her as a sister in the first place. She may have stepped up to the plate for Serenity and helped take on the responsibility for Lil Sky, but none of that would matter. She would bury her regardless. In fact, I could see her getting custody of Lil Sky and not giving a damn whether Serenity ever sees her again or not.

Ever since that baby was born Sky made sure none of them ever wanted for anything. Serenity didn't have to come out of her pockets for that little girl not once. Matter of fact, I don't think she's bought a single thing for Lil Sky. And that didn't even include the time Sky put into making sure that baby was taken care of. She's with her more than Serenity.

The wedge that would be driven between the two of them will be like a block of ice that never melted. The thing about Sky is that when the bitch comes out, she'll fight tooth and nail for what she believes to be right. And making sure that psycho rotted in jail would be her first goal. Regardless, there was no way she would ever allow that scumbag near that baby, father or not.

As big a problem as I knew Sky would be, my biggest concern was for Samir and Jacobi. They were two good men that would be driven to their limit all because of Serenity. Unfortunately, my sister didn't tend to think about everyone else that might be involved and the lives that would be affected because of her recklessness. Her sole focus was herself.

Truth be told, I was afraid of losing them. Not in the physical form, but to a system that didn't give a damn about locking another black man up. It wouldn't matter that they were protecting our sister from herself. It wouldn't matter that they were protecting four children from a crazed person instead of sitting idly by to see what he did or didn't do. I knew firsthand that in a court of law they wouldn't stand a chance at a murder bid, no matter who pulled the trigger.

The answer was obvious. I had to be the one to save my family, to be the voice of reason.

The same way I walk into those courtrooms and win my cases was the same way I intended to drive over to Serenity's and come out with a victory. I decided that I was going to go over there, not as her sister, but as her attorney. I pushed my personal feelings aside and went into full-fledged lawyer mode. I knew I needed to approach this situation delicately, as if I were trying to convince a jury.

Today, Serenity McMillan was not my sister, she was my client and I needed to be emotionally unattached in order to make her see the truth.

I knew that nothing with Serenity was ever black and white. She's complicated. If I were to push her too far, she would rebel. No, I had to dig really deep and come up with a strategy like I would do with any other case. It was time for me to go back to the basics.

Growing up, Serenity had always had a mind of her own, never following the rules. She was always in trouble, doing whatever it was she wanted to do. Anything that was considered forbidden, it intrigued her, pulling her in like a moth to the flame. Everything we ever did when she was growing up, it never worked. Which meant I needed to come in with a different approach.

I chose the perfect opportunity, a time when I knew the kids would be in school and Sky had the baby. This way, it would be just the two of us. No distractions. My gloves were off and I was ready to get this done and over with.

*****

"Hey, Sis, what brings you by this early?" Serenity asked as she opened the door and ushered me inside.

I immediately looked around her house, wishing so much more for my little sister. I didn't come over much because I hated her hood ass neighborhood. While it was safer than her last neighborhood, it was still ghetto. Thankfully, her car seemed to be running more stable, so I've been having her drop the kids off to me so that I could avoid being over here.

"Here," I handed her divorce papers that I'd spent half the night drawing up for her to sign before taking a seat on her couch. After reading his grounds for early release—being married to the victim—

I knew for a fact that the judge would grant his appeal. We see it all the time.

I could see the shock on her face as she glanced up from reading the papers. *Yes, sis, your secret is out. Thank God it landed in my ears before the rest of the family.*

Serenity sighed. "Savonna, what's done is done. You, nor anybody else can tell me who I can or can't love," she seethed, going straight into defense mode. I knew I needed to bring her down a notch or two so that she understood I wasn't here to argue. I only wanted to help her.

"Your kids come first in any situation, Serenity. Look how far they have come. This isn't about you, it's about them." I might not be a mother, but I'd learned that when you switch the focus onto their kids, they tend to think a little more clearly. And because I know my sister, I knew her soft spot was her children.

"I know this is hard for you and everybody else to understand, which was why I didn't say anything, but I believe he's changed. I have forgiven him and I trust that in time, everybody else will come around." *What the hell does she mean, she thinks? If she were thinking she wouldn't be married right now!* I could understand her forgiving him because she needed to do that in order to release herself. But I also knew that was me thinking like a sister.

I quickly shifted back to lawyer mode, unwilling to lose my cool while attempting to keep my tone sympathetic. "That's not for us to understand. I care about your safety and the safety of the kids. If the man tried to kill you once, what makes you think he won't try it again? Anything could cause him to snap. Are you willing to take that chance again? Are you going to stand there and honestly tell me that you're willing to put your children through that again?"

At this point I felt like I was pleading with the insane. There's no way Serenity was in her right mind. Mothers were supposed to protect their children, not put them in harm's way. If she truly loved the scumbag, why not wait until the kids were grown and out the house? They'd been through more than enough in their young lives and I knew there was no way in hell they would be okay with this.

"You want me to just throw away my marriage like it never happened? I don't know if I can do that, Savonna." Serenity started tearing up as if this man were her entire world. She was acting like he had been providing for her and had been her emotional support. In reality, he'd been everything but that. The simple fact that she wasn't being combative told me that what I was saying was getting to her.

I just might be able to break through to her.

"No, I want my sister to live! I want you and those kids to live in peace. Your children will never be comfortable with him around. But I think you know that." *Hell, I could use some peace myself. If she only knew what I had been going through,* I thought to myself. Deep down, I knew I couldn't make this about me because Serenity would just flip the script and stay married to the lunatic out of spite. And God forbid I mention anybody else in this family.

Nope, can't do it!

"He won't hurt me!" she shouted. "What would he tell his daughter if he did that?" It sounded more like Serenity was trying to convince herself. Little does she realize, that baby won't stop him from doing a damn thing. And I'm fairly certain all the other women that are in the grave thought the same thing. I'm sure if they were given a second chance, their decision would have been different.

"Sis, you are playing Russian roulette with your life and the lives of your kids! When it comes to life or death, thinking that a person won't try to kill you is never a guarantee. Especially when they've already tried. Please, Serenity, do the right thing. Sign these papers and I will make sure that his attorney gets them to him."

I personally knew his public defender, so it wouldn't be hard. Unfortunately for Iron, she was a shit attorney, only around for a paycheck. She was the type of lawyer you don't want representing you because she wouldn't fight for you. Whatever offer was on the table, she would try and convince her client to take. The less work, the more she could sit in her office, filing her nails and shopping online.

"Who else knows?" Serenity asked.

"Just the two of us. And I wouldn't have known had Tim not told me. It's nobody else's business."

"Just give me some time to think about it," she pled. It wasn't the answer that I was hoping to get. The victory that I wanted was to be walking out of here with the divorce papers signed. Still, I would take anything as long as it wasn't a no.

"You have my word that I won't say anything to anyone. Give me a call when you've made your decision." I gave her a quick hug before showing myself out. While I may not have gotten the answer I'd hoped for, I still felt good because I'd managed to keep my cool and was able to separate myself from the attachment that I have with my sister.

CHAPTER 18

SKY

Today was the day John and I were scheduled to meet with the mediator that Savonna had told us about. I'd been on edge all week in anticipation, snapping on my sons left and right. My nerves were being overworked and I needed a break.

Usually, I could hold my composure but I was failing miserably this week. Most of the time, I have a good grip on my emotions. Many would tell you I'm emotionless. However, lately, I'd found myself having a number of crying episodes. No one could have ever convinced me that it would hurt this bad to have your husband walk out on you. Though what hurt the most was that he didn't even want to return.

I can't believe that after everything we have been through, it all comes down to this. I'm actually in the process of getting a divorce from the man I'd been with most of my life, I thought in disbelief.

John and I had weathered many storms and we'd conquered them all. Together. So, it made me sad to think that this was how our story ended. For weeks, I'd been silently debating with myself.

What did I get myself into?

When I sent those papers to John, I never expected that it would lead us here. They were just supposed to let him know that I meant business, nothing more. But what does he do in return? The stubborn fool actually signed them. He agreed to divorce me. Just like that, everything I'd planned backfired on me. Here, my naïve ass was expecting him to come running through the front doors. Or at the very least, to call me. I was bluffing and this fool was serious.

That day showed me that some games just weren't worth playing.

I knew I was wrong when my entire family jumped down my throat. The problem was that I was too stubborn to listen. Instead, I insisted that this was what I wanted to do. Savonna even warned me that this was a possibility. But I was so sure that my husband would cave and come crawling back home to me. For a moment, I even considered withdrawing the paperwork. Unfortunately, by that time, John had already agreed to go forward and I didn't want to make a fool of myself by begging him to reconsider.

I really wish this was something that I could just undo, I inwardly groaned. *I should have just listened to my family when they told me I was out of my mind.*

Samir was the first one to approach me about everything that had happened. Apparently, John called him to vent after he got the papers. Samir called me later that evening to tell me that I was taking it too far. Lord, I would have loved to have been a fly on the wall for that conversation. Sadly, I'll never know exactly what that conversation consisted of because Samir would never tell me.

What he did tell me was that I needed to be careful what I was asking for, and that he knew I didn't want a divorce any more than he wanted to stop playing ball. He insisted that I go talk to my husband. He kept telling me to go and get John and bring him home. To him, it was that simple. Looking back, he was probably right. After all, he'd talked to John.

When I spoke to Serenity, she said I shouldn't have filed papers so quickly. She thought that I jumped the gun. From her point of view, it was stupid and I had no real reason to be trying to divorce him. In her eyes, John would always be her brother-in-law. I found that to be pretty damn hypocritical of her. Should I have felt the same way about Gary? Now, I'm not saying Gary was great, but she certainly wasn't doing any better since divorcing him.

Savonna thought the whole thing was ridiculous and way over the top. Of course, I tried not to take much of anything she said at face value. Not because I didn't appreciate and respect her opinion. It's just that since losing Preston, she'd changed. Her new motto on life was to on to what you had and be grateful that they're still with you.

Don't get me wrong, I understood that she was sensitive when it came to love. Who wouldn't be after going through a tragedy like that? But understanding the reasoning for her suggestions and actually taking them, were two completely different things. The one positive that did come out of our conversation was that she agreed to represent me. Though to be fair, I did make her feel obligated when I refused to use anyone else.

Now, the matriarch of the family, she was a whole other ball game. My mother was not happy with me, not that I expected her to be. Although I knew she could always be counted on to go to the extreme. When I told her the news, she actually cursed at me. My God-fearing momma actually cursed at me. I can count on about two fingers the number of times I'd actually heard that woman curse in my entire life. I will never forget her words for as long as I live.

"Sky, you have done lost your damn mind! I'm gonna pray for that mind of yours because it's warped!" Without another word, she hung up the phone.

I was so shocked I called her back and asked her if she meant to hang up on me. I got a repeat of exactly what she'd said before and another familiar *CLICK!* as the line disconnected.

I never did speak with my father about everything that was going on. I didn't feel it was necessary because I was certain my mother had taken care of that part for me. Knowing my father the way I did, I knew he wouldn't say anything to me unless I approached him directly. Regardless, I was willing to bet that he wasn't happy with my decision either. He loved and had so much respect for John. In the words of my father, *"Any man that takes care of his family is a man to keep."* And in that respect, John had never let me down. He never had a problem taking care of his family and he did it very well. He was a wonderful provider.

*****

I didn't want to be here, so I purposely showed up to the mediation late. I figured if I *had* to be here, I was going to make a grand entrance. Forget being professional, I came rolling up in there looking sexy as hell! I even had the nerve to show some cleavage in my little black dress.

The moment John saw me his eyes lit up. *Gotcha!* I thought, knowing I had him right where I wanted him. I knew my husband. I knew that if I could grab his attention, somewhere deep down inside of him, he still wanted me. Of course, that thought quickly faded once we started discussing our assets.

*****

"The problem is she wants to control everything! I ain't giving her shit!" John shouted, reneging on his previous words. When he initially left me, he said I could have everything. What happened to that? The past two hours we'd been going back and forth, neither of us getting anywhere. If anybody deserved to be bitter about the whole situation, it was me. He left me, not the other way around.

"Have you two tried counseling?" the mediator asked. I could tell she was aggravated with the situation. Everything I wanted, he was against giving it to me. I didn't feel I was asking too much. I wanted the house, my car, alimony, half of the savings, half his pension—which I was legally entitled to—and for him to pay all my lawyer fees. That seemed perfectly fair to me.

"Yes, several times. Usually, we work through our problems under one roof. However, since he decided to go sign a lease elsewhere, it makes it that much more difficult." When I first arrived, I was hurt. However, all that hurt had since turned to anger.

Maybe I didn't do the right thing after all. Lord knows I have better things to do with my time. My plan was to be long gone by now. I needed to do some grocery shopping, finish the laundry, and get the house cleaned up. When I was finished with that, I needed to catch up with Samir, since he'd taken the day off today.

John is not taking up my entire day, I silently vowed.

"Yep, I sure did! That's what happens when you put your husband last on the list! I removed myself and it's still a problem." John sounded like an overgrown kid. My life was set by priorities and regardless of what he thought, John was not in dire need or on his deathbed. It was not that serious and there was no need for him to move out of the house. I gave him a deadline to be back and he missed it. So, damn right I filed for divorce. By that point, he'd thrown his marriage to me away.

"It's not a problem if you give me what's rightfully mine." I don't know why John insisted on making this any harder than it already was. After carrying his children, pushing them out and raising them, he owed me. All those meals that I cooked, clothes that I washed and ironed. All the cleaning that I've done—he better be glad that was all that I was asking for. Not to mention the emotional distress and the obsessive cheating that I put up with over the years.

"You didn't work! You still don't work! I'm the one that went out there and busted my ass to keep the bills paid. If you keep the house, how are you going to afford it?" John slammed his hand down on the table and looked at the mediator as if he had won her over. He had clearly underestimated me. I'm a woman and we always find a way. I could go to work if that's what I needed to do, but what I would not do is sink.

"We're not really getting anywhere. You two keep going back and forth about the same things with no actual resolution. I've been doing this for many years now and I can see that neither of you really wants a divorce. What you two want is to argue. So, I'm going to excuse myself and allow you both to do just that." Without another word, the mediator got up and left John and I in the room looking stupid.

We both sat in silence looking at one another like we were on time out. I assumed the mediator was going to come back in, but it seemed as if she was done with our bullshit. *Wait until I tell Savonna that the mediator she hooked us up with bailed out on us. I mean, what kind of mediator does that?*

"How come you stopped taking my calls?" I finally asked. If I was going to get answers to the questions I had, this seemed like the perfect opportunity. He couldn't hang up on me or send me to voicemail when I was right in his face.

"Because you weren't talking about anything that I wanted to hear. When I talk, Sky, you listen but you don't actually get what I'm saying. You're selfish! You don't seem to understand that my needs need to be met too. I'm not telling you not to be there for your family, I'm just asking you to be considerate of the fact that you have a husband that needs you too." This was the most I'd been able to get out of him since the day he left.

We really need to work on our communication because that was not how I received it.

"I'll give you that. I can be selfish when it comes down to my family. But that doesn't mean you have to leave!" I wasn't going to tell him this now that we were actually communicating, but I don't take ultimatums well. It felt like he was trying to control me.

"I did what I needed to do for me. It seemed that just when we were on the right track, you took me back to a time I didn't seem to matter. I promised myself that if we ever found ourselves back there, I was leaving."

Why is he going all the way back there? I wondered as John referred back to when the boys came first in my life. He had no idea how hard it was to be a mother to two knuckleheads and still try to satisfy a third. Men just don't understand, nor do they want to try. You ask me, that's selfish.

"Would you consider coming over to the house later so that we can talk?" I really did miss my husband. More than I was willing to admit. Part of me felt empty without him.

"I can do that on one condition."

"Name it."

"I need you to make me a home cooked meal!" I chuckled, more than happy to make him a homecooked meal.

"How much time do I have?" I asked, lighting up like a Christmas tree. The errands that I had to run would have to wait because my husband was coming home. I made the decision right then and there that I would text Samir to let him know that I wasn't coming over after all. I knew he would understand.

"Not much. You may not make it out of the parking lot with that dress on," John whispered as he stood up. That was my cue that it was time to get out of here and quit wasting the court's time like the two fools that we were.

CHAPTER 19

SERENITY

As I sat watching Miles, Samir, and Jacobi talk shit while playing pool I realized that I'd never been with anyone who actually interacted with my family. For that reason, I was always the outsider at family events. Since my significant others would never join me, it was always just me and the kids. Not only was what Miles and I had very different for me, there was something about it that felt so right. Every time I saw him, heard the sound of his voice or felt his touch, I got butterflies in my stomach. I couldn't explain it, but all these feelings just somehow snuck up on me.

What Miles and I had was a friendship that grew into something way more. It wasn't expected and it wasn't planned. From the moment we met, we just clicked. And the more we hung out together, the closer we grew. One day, it just felt like I'd been struck by lightning. One minute, I was a married woman waiting for my husband to come home from jail. And now, I'm a married woman waiting for my divorce to come through with plans of marrying another man. A man that on any given day, I would have never looked twice at. It wasn't that he wasn't a nice-looking man. He was. He just wasn't my type of dude. I normally preferred the thugs. Which was probably why my life had been in such shambles.

That being said, I'm a firm believer that things happen in mysterious ways. Or should I say, God's divine plan sometimes happens when we least expect it. There's no other way to explain it.

After Savonna left, I found myself staring at those divorce papers for a good hour before my mind was totally made up. As much as I didn't want to admit it, she was right. My children would never accept Iron as their step-dad and the way I was thinking was very unrealistic.

In the end, I think it would prove to be too much for them to bear. And because of that, Iron and I would never be able to live freely and happily. I could stand losing, but I wouldn't lose my children in the process. Hell, they still didn't know that I was married to the man. And with any luck, they would never find out. One thing I'd learned over the years is that anything that couldn't be said or done in the open was wrong.

I decided to break the news to Iron that same night. I told him that I thought it was best if we divorced. All we'd been doing for the last couple of months was arguing anyway. He'd call and I'd spend almost the entire time listening to him threatening me. He'd say things like, *"Wait until I get out of here. I'm gonna fuck you up, bitch!"* Of course, I would hang up and wouldn't take his calls for a few days. When I would finally accept his call, he would be so apologetic and promise me the world. He would assure me time and time again that he would never harm me in any way and that he only said those things out of anger. Then, like clockwork, he'd get mad again and we'd be right back at square one.

That's when my sister's words came back to haunt me. *"Sis, you are playing Russian roulette with your life and the lives of your kids! When it comes to life or death, thinking that a person won't try to kill you is never a guarantee. Especially when they've already tried."*

For a while I would just ignore his threats and tell myself that he was just blowing off some steam. I felt like he was taking his frustration out on me because he was locked up. So much was going on over there at the jail and he was constantly being attacked by some of the inmates. Like a good wife, I would try and calm him down so that he wouldn't get into any trouble. I would remind him that every physical altercation added on more time and I was trying to avoid that for the both of us. After all, he had a daughter out here that he didn't even know.

Still, each conversation ended pretty much the same. Over time, I began to lose more and more respect for him. Certainly, the last thing that should have been coming out of his mouth to me was a threat on my life. You'd think he would know that since I was the reason he was in there in the first place. The sad part is that our arguments were over petty stuff. He was mad that his daughter was with Sky, mad that I missed his phone call, mad that I couldn't afford to put money on his books.

Eventually, I came to believe that if he couldn't keep himself humble enough to stay on my good side while he was locked up, then there was nothing to stop him from shooting me again. And who knows, the next time he very well may have succeeded in killing me. Or, God forbid, my kids.

I tried to convince myself that he was this changed person and that he would never hurt the mother of his daughter—all the things that I wanted to believe. Sadly, that just wasn't the truth. Even before Savonna showed up at my door, I was having second thoughts about staying married to him. The only reason I was holding on was because I didn't want to fail again. For once in my life, I wanted to win. Mentally, I felt I had something to prove to myself. And I had every intention of showing everyone that I was right—love does conquer all!

That was until one weekend I went to drop the kids off at Savonna's and I had an epiphany. I had gone inside to kick it with her for a little bit and Savonna said to me, *"Serenity, what's going on? You're so happy. I haven't seen you like this since we were kids."* I didn't respond to her at the time because I hadn't even noticed it myself.

However, as I was driving back home it just so happened that Miles called. The moment I saw his name flash across my scream I could feel myself smile. Truly smile. It was then that I realized he was the reason I'd been so happy. Miles had unexpectedly brought the joy back into my life. Still, I was stubborn.

Even after my revelation I fought my feelings. I told myself that there was no way it could be true. Yet, with each phone call I accepted from Iron, nothing he said could get under my skin. Which was definitely not like me. Normally, I would have been stressed out and pissed off. Then again, I didn't exactly have time to be pissed off because I was too busy chatting it up with Miles in my free time. Talking to him changed me. He helped to bring out the best in me.

I literally told that man everything and he has never once judged me. He constantly encourages me. He's my nourishment, the cleansing to my soul. Because of him, I was confident in myself again. He's patient, understanding—everything I never knew I needed.

I know it sounds a bit cliché, but that man was made for me and I'd never been more in love. I couldn't wait to be his wife.

When Miles and I initially discussed it, he told me I could have anything I wanted. Well, since my first two weddings were in jails, I didn't exactly have the highest standards. It took a bit of convincing––myself, mainly—but I decided that if I was going to get married, my last wedding was going to be a big one, in the church, with a massive reception to follow.

The plan was for me and the kids to move to Charlotte with Miles. Since he was already established, it didn't make much sense for him to relocate to D.C. and have to start from scratch. Plus, I could use a different atmosphere. Honestly, he could have been in Alaska and I still would have gone. Though, for now, we were doing the long-distance thing, ensuring we saw each other twice a month. I would go down there one weekend out of the month and he would come here one weekend out of the month. That would continue until my divorce was finalized.

What made Miles that much more special was that he refused to make love to me until I was divorced. Initially, I didn't believe him. I figured I would be able to change his mind. Nope, no such luck. Instead, I got my feelings hurt. Miles was the first man to ever turn me down and it felt like I was being punished. Needless to say, I couldn't wait for my divorce to come through.

Until then, Miles has made his biggest mission to bond with my children. He wanted to earn their trust and respect. Which was proving to be a real challenge. When we were just friends, the kids were fine. But now that we were an official couple, they weren't feeling it.

After everything they had been through, I knew it was going to take my kids a good minute to get used to me having someone in my life. In our lives. The last man they were around was Iron and we all saw how that turned out. Thankfully, Miles understood and wasn't trying to force it. I knew they would eventually like him. Until then, it was like pulling teeth.

When Miles comes over, they sit and stare at him sideways. My boys remain on guard at all times and Serene acts like she's my mother. In an effort to show the kids that he was serious about being with us, he would come over and spend the day with us before leaving to return to his hotel at a decent hour. I hated every time he would leave me but I knew he couldn't stay. Not if he intended to truly earn my children's trust.

Once the kids were in bed for the evening, I would call and the two of us would talk the rest of the night away. Another quality that I loved about Miles. We never seemed to run out of things to talk about. One minute, we could be talking about politics, the weather or traumas in our past life. The next, we would be laughing over the stupidest stuff. This man was so in tune to my feelings that he would sit and cry or laugh with me. We could talk for hours before eventually falling asleep together while on the phone. Which was something I hadn't done since I was a kid, sneaking to talk to my boyfriend long after my parents had gone to bed.

But, like everyone, Miles wasn't perfect. He had some bad traits that I didn't particularly care for. Right off the bat I noticed that he could be clingy and a bit insecure. To some people, that may not have been a problem. However, I was the type of woman that needed her space every now and then. I could only hope that things would change once I moved to Charlotte. With Miles at work, and me planning to go back to work, we'll have more than enough time to miss one another.

As for his insecurity…I could kind of understand it. When we decided to move forward, Miles had me change my number so that Iron couldn't get in touch with me. Deep down, I knew it was his way of protecting me and the kids. However, he also needed to have a little faith. I told him time and time again that he had nothing to worry about. And he didn't. Even if I were to entertain my jailbird husband it would only be to tell him about my plans for Lil Sky. Regardless, I wasn't going anywhere.

One night, Miles and I were talking about the kids when he asked me how I would feel about him formally adopting Lil Sky and assuming the role of her father. I was stunned. I couldn't have picked a better father for my children. Miles and I both agreed that we would tell her about her biological father when she was older. For the time being, we thought it best to keep her as far asway from Iron as possible. For her own well-being.

I wanted all of my children to feel loved. And at the moment, Sky was being left out. Gary did his part with the other three. He'd even been consistently paying his child support. However, when he would come to pick them up, Lil Sky would put her hands up, as if begging him to take her too. It broke my heart every single time.

While we were on the subject, I informed Miles that I would get my tubes untied so that we could have one or two of our own. His next words were just another example of the reason I loved him so much.

"Only if that's what you want to do. I don't ever want to put you through any pain. Nothing in life is that important." He was so sweet and genuinely concerned for my safety.

*****

"Sis? Sis? Sister!" Savonna yelled, pulling me from my thoughts.

"Yes?" I asked, startled. I had nearly forgotten that she said she was on her way to the pool hall. I asked her to come because I needed some girl time. Cassey was at home getting dinner ready and Sky had the baby, so I couldn't call either of them.

"What in the world has you in such a daze?" Savonna asked as she took a seat next to me waving to Samir, Jacobi, and Miles.

"Miles," I murmured while looking straight at him. *Damn I got a man this time, a real one.*

"Awww, I'm so happy to finally see you happy!" Savonna hugged me. She couldn't have been happier with my choice of a man. No more thug life for me. From now on, I was going to accept that I deserved better.

"Any news on my divorce yet?" I asked, anxious to get it over with. In truth, I couldn't wait to have sex again. It had certainly been a minute.

"Look at you, rushing the process," Savonna chuckled. "I haven't' heard anything yet, but I'm confident it will be coming soon." She knew my struggle and how mad I was at Miles when he turned me down. I actually called Savonna and asked her if she thought the man was gay.

"Where's your sidekick?" I asked, referring to Chad.

Savonna and I had been having a number of heart-to-heart conversations about him. I really think he might be the one for her. The only thing holding her back was her. She had to be willing to open her heart up. And so far, she hasn't. It felt like every time I saw her, I was begging her to give him another chance. Happiness was right around the corner for my sister. I could feel it.

"Working, I believe. Speaking of Chad, I've been thinking a lot about what you said. Seeing all of you so happy has me wondering if maybe I'm missing out." *Thank God, she is finally coming around. I'd been praying for this for what felt like an eternity. My sister will not be an old maid after all,* I thought excitedly.

"So, you're finally going to give Chad a chance?" I asked, tears welling in my eyes. All I could do was cry because there was nothing I wanted more than for Savonna to be happy again.

"Awwww, you're crying!" she said, wiping a tear from my cheek. "And yes, I think I'm ready to love again. Like you, I believe Chad is the man for me." I grabbed Savonna and embraced her as tears ran down both of our cheeks. This was the moment that we'd all been waiting and praying for.

I can't wait to tell everyone the good news! Savonna McMillan is open to love again.

CHAPTER 20

SAVONNA

Today is the day, I assured myself as I mentally checked everything off of my list. I'd spent the last several days planning a nice little date for Chad and I in the park. Normally, I wouldn't have been so nervous—I'd always been comfortable around Chad—but this was different. Today, I was going to tell him that I was ready to move forward with him. Before leaving the house, I decked my apartment out in rose petals and candles ready to be lit. I'd even set out a sexy red negligee on the bed.

Hurrying out to the door, I wanted to make sure I had enough time to find the perfect little spot where we could be alone. It only took a few minutes before I found a nice little spot underneath a big, beautiful tree that I thought suited the two of us. Quickly laying the blanket out, I got to work unpacking the picnic basket I'd filled with the sushi that I'd picked up on the way, which I paired with our favorite wine and two glasses.

Yeah, you could say I was pretty confident about how this date was going to go. Sadly, nothing in my life ever goes according to plan.

Just as I was about to tell Chad that I thought he was the man for me, he informed me that he met someone he was very interested in. It felt like a bomb had gone off inside my chest. *I should have never let Serenity get into my head,* I thought, my heart breaking all over again. *I should have known this would happen. I'm not meant to find love.*

Oblivious to my inner turmoil, Chad continued to go on and on about this new woman he'd met and wonderful she was. In an effort to avoid breaking down in front of him, I avoided eye contact as I stared up into the air, my mind wandering.

What a complete waste of time! I spent half my day getting prepared for yet another disappointment. Such is the story of my life. By now, I should be used to it.

After what felt like an eternity, Chad took in our surroundings. "This is so nice," he muttered before his eyes settled on the sushi. I watched as a wide grin spread across his face. "Oh, we're getting fancy now." It was clear he thought this was just another one of our many dates that went go on.

I spent the rest of our 'date' in embarrassed misery. The last place I wanted to be was sitting in front of the man I was prepared to move forward with before finding out that he was interested in another woman. It couldn't have ended soon enough.

*****

That evening, when I was telling Serenity everything that had happened, she said I should have cut him off and told him how I felt. I didn't tell her, but I disagreed. If Chad and I were on the same page, like I'd originally thought, he would have noticed the difference.

To be fair, he did ask me what was wrong a couple of times. I didn't want to get in my feelings so I told him that I was fine. Of course, if he hadn't been so excited about his new love interest, he would have noticed that I was completely full of shit.

Now I understood how he felt when I kept turning him down. It didn't feel good at all. Though I guess it could have been worse. I could have told him how I felt and he could have turned me down. At least this way, he doesn't know how I really feel.

Ever since Chad begun pursuing this other woman, I hadn't seen him. Another thing I used to do to him—blow him off. Lately, any time I would call he was busy or going on a date. That shit stung. But what hurt the most was when he told me he wanted me to meet her. I wasn't interested, but what was I supposed to do, be phony? Maybe once I've gotten over the pain and embarrassment I was feeling, but that time hadn't come yet. One thing was for sure, I would get over this. Worse has happened and I was still standing.

Now, to make matters worse, I had to go meet Angel and Danielle for lunch at Joe's Seafood. They were both adamant and said they had good news for me. Lord knows I needed some good news.

Lately, it seemed their rocky marriage was blossoming. Angel was no longer complaining and often boasted about the things they were doing in life. I swear, everyone around me was happy except me. Don't get me wrong, I wasn't hating. I just wished I had some good news to share with everyone else as well.

Serenity, mess that she is, signed the divorce papers I'd dropped off and everything was finalized the other day. Just as I'd promised, I never mentioned her little prison marriage to anyone else in the family. Which proved to be a good decision because she and Miles announced that they were planning on getting married. Everyone was ecstatic. Of course, Serenity asked me to be the maid of honor.

And that was only the beginning of the happiness surrounding me.

Jacobi and Tamela recently discovered they were expecting their first child together. None of us were surprised when they asked Cassey and Samir to be the godparents. I was so happy for them. I decided this was the perfect opportunity to plan an over-the-top baby shower.

John and Sky had put their bullshit behind them and decided to renew their vows. Like the first time they got married, I am acting as the maid of honor.

In addition, my nephews were also doing well. Prince's baby mama went forward with the charges she was trying to hit him with. As promised, I managed to get all charges dropped against Prince. Luckily for her, the judge was feeling generous. He was initially going to lock her up on perjury charges. In the end, he let her crying ass go. But not before informing her that he was ordering full custody of their son be granted to Prince.

Everyone was pleased with the way things turned out, but no one was more pleased than John and Sky. They knew he would need help caring for the baby while he was at work, so they stepped up and were picking up any slack. The only downside to the judge's ruling was that LaWanda had been granted visitation every other weekend and alternating holidays.

Not long after his day in court, Prince met a nice young lady that Sky actually adored. I never thought I would see the day.

Profit and his long time Boo had recently gotten engaged and moved into a place of their own. I still think they're too young to be talking about getting married, but that's not my decision to make. Look at John and Sky…they made it work. Which is exactly the point I have to keep making when Sky goes off the deep end. Both boys were happy, which meant I was happy. I couldn't be more proud of the young men they had grown up to be. They turned their lives around and never looked back.

*****

"Hello?" I answered without even looking at my phone.

"Girl, where are you?" Angel asked. "You're supposed to meet us at twelve!" I looked at the time on my computer and was shocked to find that it was twelve fifteen.

"You told me 1 o'clock, but whatever. I'm on my way. I'll be there in five minutes," I said, disconnecting the call. I know I could be a bit scattered, but I was certain she told me 1 o'clock, and I had the text to prove it.

It's a good thing I don't have that far to walk, I thought to myself as I grabbed my purse and hurried out of the office.

I stepped outside to find that it was a beautiful day. I was enjoying the warm breeze as I walked the couple of blocks to the restaurant. I hadn't made it very far when I spotted a man who appeared homeless slumped over in the corner. However, the closer I got to him the more familiar he became.

"Darius?" I muttered unintentionally.

"Savonna!" he shouted, turning to face me with a smile upon his face. If I were him, I wouldn't have wanted anyone to know that it was me. I would have simply ignored them and prayed they kept going.

"How's it going?" From the looks of things, it wasn't going too well. He looked horrible.

"I'm not doing too good. I've been homeless for that last couple of months. I'm so sorry for what I did to you," Darius apologized while reaching out to grab me. Panicked, I jumped backward.

"Don't be, I'm good. I'll keep you in my prayers." Without another word, I walked away and didn't bother looking back. *Thank you, God, for saving me,* I silently prayed, grateful the bum had done me the way he did.

Now that was a whole mood changer. All my ex's are called ex's for a reason. I didn't miss out on anything. Looking back, I could smack myself in the face for crying over Darius. However, what I just experienced was a big dose of reality. The odd thing is that I had just been thinking about him last week. I figured he was probably married with children, living the good life.

That's when a thought struck me. *He very well could be married. Oh, goodness! If he is married, I feel bad for his poor wife. I just hope like hell that he's not somebody's father. That would be a real disaster.*

When I reached my destination, I glanced around the restaurant and quickly found Angel waving at me from the corner. I walked over and took a seat at the table. "Hey, ladies, what's going on?"

"What took you so long? I was just about to call you!" Angel asked, her tone snappy. *I would have been on time had you given me the correct time,* I thought to myself in irritation.

"It doesn't even matter. I'm here now!" I started to tell her that I'd run into Darius, but I quickly realized he wasn't worth my breath.

Just then, the waitress appeared. "Do you all need a few more minutes to look over the menu?" she asked.

"No, I think we're ready," I responded after seeing Angel and Danielle shaking their heads. I was here so often that I already knew what I wanted. "Can I get the crab dip and a lemonade," I asked.

"Of course." She finished writing down my order before turning to address Angel and Danielle. "What can I get for you ladies?"

"Could we get the crab cake special to share, please?"

"Absolutely. I'll go put this in and be right back with your lemonade," she assured before disappearing in the direction of the kitchen.

"We know that you're a very busy woman," Angel began as soon as the waitress was out of ear shot. "We know that you have a lot going on—" *What are these two trying to hint at?* I wondered.

"Just tell her, Angel!"

I smiled as the waitress set my drink down in front of me before sauntering off. "Yes, just tell me!" Angel knew how much I hated when people would beat around the bush.

"Okay, Okay—WE'RE PREGNANT! You're going to be a godmother!" My mouth fell wide open when Danielle stood up to show me her baby bump.

I was stunned and needed answers as to how this could have happened. Danielle was the more masculine of the duo, and she'd never wanted anything to do with a man. Angel, on the other hand, had been with both sexes. If one of them was going to be having a baby I would have expected it to be Angel.

"H–How did this happen?" I stammered. Nowadays, I knew women didn't necessarily need a man to have a baby. But if you weren't gonna have a man, you damn sure need a lot of money. And those two were not balling like that.

Apparently, Angel had given Danielle permission to sleep with her best friend, Dave, in order to get pregnant. Sure enough, she's now three months along. I didn't bother asking how many times they'd slept together because I was still in a state of shock. For obvious reasons. Angel was known for being very jealous and Danielle didn't even like penis.

I shook my head as I tried to process everything I'd just been told. *This is the most bizarre shit I've ever heard.*

We spent the next hour talking about the baby, how she'd been feeling since falling pregnant, and just generally catching up. When we had finished, we paid our bills and parted ways. But not before I agreed to be the baby's godmother. While I was curious about the intimate details, I decided to wait until Angel came to me.

*****

I walked back to my office in a trance-like state, my mind racing with thoughts. While I was happy for my friends, I was still very confused.

Just then, I heard a familiar voice calling my name, pulling me from my thoughts. "Savonna, Savonna!"

When I turned around, my breath hitched in my throat and I felt like I couldn't breathe. Standing there before me was a ghost from my past. *This can't be. How is this possible.* My eyes filled with tears and I couldn't speak as he approached with a wide smile on his face.

"I'm home, baby, I got an early release!" Adonis called out as he scooped me into his arms and held me up in the air.

EPILOGUE

SAVONNA

Life had sure thrown me some curve balls and played with my heart a million times over. Still, through many lessons and tests, I conquered them all. Even when I thought I wasn't going to make it, I persevered. I never thought I would be able to love again, not in the same way I loved Preston. But with Adonis, it was like a blast from my past.

I can admit that he was that one ex that left with us with unfinished business. We never had a real clear ending. However, we did have another beautiful beginning.

Like a bright light in my dark world, Adonis swooped in just when I needed him most. Now, happily married, it finally feels like I am on the right path. I'd had the wedding of my dreams, all of my family and friends present, and now we were expecting our very first child. After all this time, I was finally going to be a mother. With Adonis, I no longer focused on the past, only my future.

And it was certainly looking bright.

Serenity finally got her head right and ended up marrying Miles. She and the kids moved to Charlotte and everyone seemed to be doing well, all glory to God. She's even got a job working at the Department of Social Services helping young women like herself.

Tamela and Jacobi recently welcomed beautiful twin girls, Mirrah and Miranda. Yes, Jacobi nearly passed out when he found out they were having twins. But just as we all expected, he fell right into line and is a wonderful, doting father.

Sky and John finally put all their issues aside and were enjoying their empty nest.

As for Mom and Dad, they are doing well, happy that all four of their children are happily married and doing well.

OTHER BOOKS BY STACEY FENNER

A TOXIC LOVE AFFAIR
Available at: Amazon

Tyrone and Daniel are two best friends but total opposites. Tyrone has his woman at home taking care of the kids while he's out playing in the streets. He soon finds out that being too comfortable and secure will cost him everything when he comes home to an empty home.

Will his womanizing ways wreck his life or can he get it together before it's to late?

Daniel on the other hand, is still trying to heal from a messy divorce with Candace five years later. He's tried dating but finds it hard to move on.

Find out what happens with a good-looking man who has money to buy everything but is unfulfilled on the inside. A Toxic Love Affiar is filled with love, lust, hate and drama.

*****

A TOXIC LOVE AFFAIR 2
Available at: Amazon

They say once a good girl is gone she's gone forever, and if you thought Part 1 threw you for a loop, then get ready to do figure 8's this go around.

Belinda sets out on a mission to destroy all her childhood, so-called, friends that have betrayed her. She has no boundaries or limits to her destruction. She has intentions on making each and every one of them pay, and has masterminded a plan that will eventually cause her to self-destruct in the worst way!

Being disloyal to Belinda will cost them everything. Everybody likes to play but nobody wants to pay!

Meanwhile, Daniel finally opens himself up to love again after going through his messy divorce with his scandalous ex-wife, Candace. That won't last too long when a jealous Candace gets wind of the relationship; she throws a monkey wrench trying to exhaust him of all hope. Meanwhile, Daniel is stuck cleaning up the mess Tyrone created.

Find out if Tyrone and Daniel's friendship can survive the aftermath when Daniel gets wind to what Belinda is up to and he feels responsible for her trifling ways. Shocked is an understatement as to how he feels about a woman he once had so much respect for.

*****

A TOXIC LOVE AFFAIR 3
Available at: Amazon

These toxic relationships will take it to another level of trifling in this final installment of the Toxic Love Series.

Tyrone takes a trip back down memory lane and reunites with his drug-addicted mother on a quest to find out who his father is. After hooking up with Dana, Daniel's sister, Tyrone decides to turn in his player card and be a father to all of the children that he has fathered, but karma has a funny way of landing right back in his lap. Getting what he gave in life; will trouble from the past overcome him?

Daniel relocates back to Atlanta to be with Shaunda, the woman that he plans on spending the rest of his life with, but an unexpected visitor will come along and be the interruption of everything. Meanwhile, Shaunda reveals another side of herself that has Daniel questioning her pure existence. As Daniel's hatred toward his ex-best friend, Mr. Tyrone himself, grows after he learns of the secret relationship of Tyrone and Dana.

Sheree and Calvin's marriage is on the rocks once again because of Sheree's obsession in finding Belinda to seek revenge. Sheree bites off more than she can handle when another secret of hers is revealed.

Belinda makes her way back to the states and right back into the arms of her protector, Troy. But of course not without a twist to her madness.

Rivals will come face to face when a funeral places everyone in the same location…but who will meet their untimely demise?

*****

THE COMMANDMENTS OF A FEMALE HUSTLER

Available at: Amazon

Meet the well-known trio, Lala, Binky and Jay, who been rocking and rolling together since their childhood days. Raised in the projects these three had only one thing on their minds, the come up! These ladies will show you how to use what you got to get what you want!

What starts out as 'may the best woman win' ends in a rage of jealousy, dividing the three. After such a betrayal, can their relationship be fixed? What happens when the commandments are no longer followed? One will find love, one will end up behind bars, and one's mind is sick and twisted!

Swift, Jock, and Moose have the east side of Baltimore locked down with the drug game, but stuff gets twisted when there's a murder involved. When relationships fail, sex, lies and love take over. Their loyalty towards one another will be tested in the worst way. Rivals will meet, love will be found and hearts will be changed as the hustler game is taken to a whole new level of disrespect!

Who will be the sell out?

*****

THE COMMANDMENTS OF A FEMALE HUSTLER 2

Available at: Amazon

"

The worst thing a woman can do is bank on her looks. Lala will soon find out that beauty is only skin deep in the worst way! When you're a woman with no substance that carries a torch around filled with nothing but attitude, people tend to turn on you and you become as ugly as you are on the inside!

With Swift, Rock, and Sweets locked up in Chesapeake Detention Center, facing hundreds of years, Moose assumes the role of *Head Man in Charge.* Letting all the power go to his head, treating Lala like his intern, these two will clash, as they both suffer from control issues.

Jay's dream relationship with Boss is crashing down around her. The duo had it all, but as he goes downhill, he takes Jay right along for the ride! Stuck with three kids that don't belong to her, and taking care of her Grandmother, money is tight, leaving her no other choice but to go back to her old ways!

Running from Baltimore, with goals in mind of her and Jay living out their dreams of owning their own shop, Binky moves in with Jay to start her life over. Her love life takes off, headed in the right direction, but bad decisions will be her downfall, leaving her devastated and distraught!

Tighten your seatbelt and get ready for these twists and turns!

*****

THE COMMANDMENTS OF A FEMALE HUSTLER 3
Available at: Amazon

Lala is back—and she's back with a vengeance! From an overpriced whore, sold to the highest bidder, to Queen Pin…just like the devil she's out to kill and destroy! Her sick, twisted mind and love for the dollar has her believing that she has a PhD in the street hustle! Will she end up leading herself to a fatal destruction?

Binky and Jay tried to leave B-more behind them and focus on their future in LA, unfortunately, life won't allow them to forget their roots! A storm is brewing as life-long secrets are revealed! Will the once trio, turned duo, be able to weather the storm?

Swift is getting burnt out and rethinking his life after all of the responsibility of handling the territories of his once archenemies, Sweets and Rock. With a sound mind he feels it's time to make a change and get out of the business!

But is it really that easy?

Every good man needs a good woman to bring out the best in him! From the side dish to the main dish, Swift's gem has that effect on him! Diamond is planning their wedding, in hopes of soon bearing his children, and the future's looking bright.

Unfortunately for them, Lala will have none of it.

*****

New Haven Ratchet Business
Available at: Amazon

There's a lot that goes on in the small city of New Haven. Where the men have it their way, and prey on a woman's weaknesses!

Let me introduce you to the Bum Squad, which consists of Poncho, the ringleader, Rich, Quan, Mickey and Trey! Ladies, stay away from these types of men! Bums they are. They don't work, but manage to have all their needs and wants supplied by the women that they choose to date! These five men have it all with nothing to give!

Poncho is the dirtiest of them all, reeling women in, only to suck the life out of them, leaving them broken-hearted and confused! Rich, the washed up has-been finds himself stuck in a family affair that will have two cousins at each other's throats! Quan, Mickey, and Trey seem to understand their lane. They're not looking for much, just a place to lay their heads!

Liz and Chris are archenemies, both having a history with the infamous Poncho! Poncho does Chris in, leaving her suicidal and bitter! Liz runs to the rescue to dig her out of the pit of hell that she's mentally in!

Dominique and Keisha will face off over Rich and his lies of deceit. A gullible Mika will find herself involved in the trifecta love affair, as she becomes victim to Rich and his lies!

Find out what happens in the Ratchet New Haven Business.

*****

NEW HAVEN RATCHET BUSINESS 2
Available at: Amazon

With no intentions of letting any of his women down, no other man can top the swag of Mr. Poncho. He is for sure putting it on the ladies. He can duck and dodge his way out of any situation and now that is being put to the test. Find out what happens when his lies become his truth and he finds himself planning two weddings at the same time.

Chris tries her best to move on and suppress her feelings for Poncho. While the dating scene seems like the right thing to do to occupy her mind, she will find herself running into plenty of brick walls! Weak to Poncho and his long stroke, he's coming on strong and has her believing that he's been reformed to be everything that she has ever wanted in a man. Will she believe him and leave all her insecurities in the past?

Liz and Tyson's relationship is tested once again when friendships play a very big part. Tyson finds himself running in second place, while Liz is too consumed with her friends and not him. Will Liz choose her needy friends over Tyson or will she choose him?

Rich tries his hardest to prove his love for Dominique and repair the marriage that he messed up, unfortunately it looks like he's in it by himself, and Dominique has already checked out. However, juggling his triangle of love affairs comes with unexpected surprises!

Just when you thought things couldn't get any worse…

*****

New Haven Ratchet Business 3
Available at: Amazon

The Bum Squad hasn't been the same since Rich and Quan began growing and realizing that there's more to life than living off of women. While they are reaching for something better, the other three are looking from afar—still being the bums that they are!

Poncho is like a disease that you can't get rid of, the poison to a woman's soul that sticks like glue. Running his same game, promising to turn over a new leaf and change his ways with no intention of doing either. He's happy doing him and all the women in his life that he chooses to deceive, but not before adding to the list of women that are addicted to his long stroke!

Chris is the happiest that she's ever been in her life. She's living the life that she always dreamed of, determined that nothing or no one will come and break up her happy home.

Giving love another shot, Liz and Tyson are a match made in heaven. Like any other couple, things get a little rocky when Tyson gets tired and gets a little loose at the lips. Once again it becomes a battleground!

Friendships will be tested, loyalty revoked, and relationships will crumble as New Haven becomes smaller than it already is!

*****

New Haven Ratchet Business 4
Available at: Amazon

The Ratchetness in New Haven Continues!

The bum Squad is living their best life all except Poncho, he hits an all-time low when his long stroke is no longer able to conquer his quest! His hitlist is running on E! Forcing him to make some decisions in his life! Will he change for the better or continue his manipulating lying ways?

Chris is once again is left broken hearted and distraught by Poncho! Focused on putting the pieces of her life back together, her suicidal ways makes her turn to Tyson the only real friend that she feels she has! Can the now mother of two really be over Poncho?

Tyson and Liz just can't seem to get it together! As their relationship crumbles, Liz is torn between doing what's right or letting Poncho sink! Is she going to help Poncho raise his baby at her own expense? Will her heart allow her to see the father of her children out in the streets?

*****

NEW HAVEN RATCHET BUSINESS 5
Available at: Amazon

This is the finale of the New Haven Ratchet Business Series!

It's getting serious in New Haven as the Bum Squad decides to run an illegal afterhours for a come up! Rich tries to warn them, all money ain't good money!

Poncho uses the after hour as a cover up for his women, there are more babies to come and more women on his hit list! When will he learn?

Rich has thrown in his player card, he makes a conscious decision to give up on women forever! Being by himself gives him peace of mind!

Chris finally runs into a decent man that loves and adores her but is he enough to take away her itch from Poncho?

Sweet old Liz decides to try her hand at the dating scene, read to see if she finds her happily ever after!

*****

LOVE DON'T LOVE ME 1
Available at: Amazon

Meet the McMillian's!

This close-knit family seems like they have it all together. Sky, Samir, Serenity, and Savonna all come from two very religious parents. They were raised with high standards, morals, and values! What goes on behind closed doors, stays behind closed doors!

Sky the oldest of them all, has built this illusion of her picture-perfect family! Married to her long-time husband John, raising two young men who are everything but saints! Sky vows to keep up with the image and facade of being happily married! What looks good on the outside doesn't match what's going on the inside!

Samir is a prime example of a superficial man. Cassey looks good on the arm but beauty is only temporary when a woman doesn't have much to offer other than that! Samir is neglected and under appreciated by his gold-digging wife who refuses to lift a finger other than shop! If only he could go back to his college days and un-wife his wife!

Serenity, the rebellious one, walks to her own beat! The only rules she follows are her own. A repeat offender of being addicted to the bad boy, laced with the opposite of her sisters' and brother. Married to ex-convict, Gary, this struggling mother of three gets quite fed up with her jobless husband!

Savonna the successful Attorney at law, has it all together, easy on the eye, self-sufficient, confidant, seems to have it all but the one thing she longs for! Love, Marriage, and a family of her own! All she seems to encounter are failed relationships and broken promises! She can't find Mr. Right if her life depended on it! Feeling defeated until she runs into Mr. Adonis who gives her hope of a healthy future and longevity! Could he be the one?

All the McMillians in their own right have the right to say— Love Don't Love Me!

*****

LOVE DON'T LOVE ME 2
Available at: Amazon

Savonna finds herself battling depression and having panic attacks from the side effects of Adonis. Just when she thought she'd found her soulmate, she ended up broken-hearted and distraught! Once again defeated by love, she wants nothing more than to close up her heart! Unfortunately, her ticking biological clock and timeline nearing, she realizes that isn't an option if she wants the things she always planned for her life.

When the truth is revealed and the lie exposed, roles reverse between Samir and Jacobi. The lifelong bachelor tries his hand at love with Tamela while Samir is having a hard time holding onto his marriage with Cassey! If only he had remembered, 'what's done in the dark always comes to the light!'

As it turns out, the key to John and Sky's marriage was time away from their troublesome sons. No longer faking it to make it, their love is real and they are once again enjoying one another! Building their way to a solid foundation with the help of marriage counselor, Sky is slowly letting John take the lead as head of the household!

Tragedy comes knocking when Serenity tries her hand at trifling! Newly divorced, her life begins spiraling out of control while playing with two demon seeds that share the same DNA!

Sibling rivalry, tested love, ultimate betrayal—can the McMillian's keep their strong family dynamic or will all be for naught?

About Stacey Fenner

Instagram: authorstaceyfenner
Twitter: sfenner1
Facebook: www.facebook.com/authorstaceyfenner

You can contact Stacey Fenner at
authorstaceyfenner@gmail.com

Stacey Fenner, was born December 1 and raised in New Haven, CT., the youngest of three. In 1999 Stacey relocated to Atlanta, GA where she resided for a year before moving to Baltimore, MD to care for her parents with her two daughters.

Writing since she was a child was a way to express herself, allowing her to overcome many trials and tribulations. However, she never pursued her gift until 2008. Although she obtained her degree in accounting, and currently works in that field, her passion is and always has been writing.

Stacey's writing career is focused upon novels about relationships. Her first book, A Toxic Love Affair, which was published in April of 2015, landed her in the #37 spot on the Woman's Urban Best Selling list. Her follow-up novel, A Toxic Love Affair Part 2, landed in the # 24 spot on that very same list. Having just recently finished up Part 3 of that series, Stacey is taking the Indie world by storm.